WICKED WILL

A Mystery of Young William Shakespeare

BAILEY MacDONALD

Aladdin

NEW YORK LONDON TORONTO SYDNEY

If you purchased this book without a cover, you should be aware that this book is stolen property. It was reported as "unsold and destroyed" to the publisher, and neither the author nor the publisher has received any payment for this "stripped book."

This book is a work of fiction. Any references to historical events, real people, or real locales are used fictitiously. Other names, characters, places, and incidents are the product of the author's imagination, and any resemblance to actual events or locales or persons, living or dead, is entirely coincidental.

ALADDIN
An imprint of Simon & Schuster Children's Publishing Division
1230 Avenue of the Americas, New York, NY 10020
First Aladdin paperback edition October 2010
Copyright © 2009 by Brad Strickland
All rights reserved, including the right of reproduction in whole or in part in any form.
ALADDIN is a trademark of Simon & Schuster, Inc., and related logo is a registered trademark of Simon & Schuster, Inc.
Also available in an Aladdin hardcover edition.
For information about special discounts for bulk purchases, please contact Simon & Schuster Special Sales at 1-866-506-1949 or business@simonandschuster.com.
The Simon & Schuster Speakers Bureau can bring authors to your live event.
For more information or to book an event contact the Simon & Schuster Speakers Bureau at 1-866-248-3049 or visit our website at www.simonspeakers.com.
Designed by Mike Rosamilia
The text of this book was set in Hoefler Text.
Manufactured in the United States of America 0810 OFF
2 4 6 8 10 9 7 5 3 1
The Library of Congress has cataloged the hardcover edition as follows:
MacDonald, Bailey.
Wicked Will / by Bailey MacDonald.—1st Aladdin ed.
p. cm.
Summary: Performing in the English town of Stratford-on-Avon in 1576, a young actress (disguised as a boy) and a local lad named Will Shakespeare uncover a murder mystery.
ISBN 978-1-4169-8660-7 (hc)
1. Shakespeare, William, 1564–1616—Childhood and youth—Juvenile fiction.
[1. Shakespeare, William, 1564–1616—Childhood and youth—fiction.
2. Theater—Fiction. 3. Disguise—Fiction. 4. Orphans—Fiction. 5. Great Britain—History—Elizabeth, 1558–1603—Fiction. 6. Mystery and detective stories.] I. Title.
PZ7.M14637Wi 2009
[Fic]—dc22
2008050818
ISBN 978-1-4169-8661-4 (pbk)
ISBN 978-1-4169-8724-6 (eBook)

To a fantastic writer
who's always willing to help,
Tom Deitz

The Most Woeful Comedy
and Humorous Tragedy

WICKED WILL

(or, *Murder in Stratford*)

⚘ One ⚘

"The best actors in the world . . ."

The night before had shrieked with wind and boomed with thunder, but dawn broke rain-washed and cool. We strolling players had no inkling that another and much worse kind of storm lay ahead. Indeed, that June morning in 1576 struck us all as a good omen, fair weather following foul.

Since before sunrise our wagon had been rumbling along toward Stratford-on-Avon. Bright woolly clouds drifted across the sky like white sheep grazing the hills of high heaven. From the trees on either side of the road cuckoos sent their double calls floating on the air. Even when the sun stood directly overhead, the day felt cool for June, and the four members of our acting company who had to amble along behind the wagon, Watkyn Bishop,

Peter Stonecypher, Alan Franklin, and Michael Moresby, did not complain, though to be sure by noon they had long since ceased to sing their jolly walking songs. The wagon, crammed with our costumes and properties, held only my uncle, Matthew Bailey, old Ben Fadger, and me.

Or it *had* held me, until a mile back on the road, when Uncle Matthew had taken up the local boy who called himself Will to be our guide. Nearly a year of acting had introduced me to audiences both rude and civil, made up of all sorts of people young and old, but the main point about audiences was that they usually listened more than they spoke. Such was not true of Will, and he wouldn't take my stubborn silences or irritated shrugs as answers to his questions.

The boy, who had a plain face under an untidy thatch of brown hair, began with, "I'm called Will. What's your name?"

I saw my uncle's red face twitch in a pleading wink, asking me to suffer this prying boy's curiosity.

"Thomas Pryne," I said, adding no more because I had no wish to encourage his chat.

But he would not take a hint. "How old are you?"

"Twelve," I said shortly. That was a lie, for I was within days of turning fourteen, but 'twas a lie my uncle wanted me to tell.

"So am I! I was twelve this April past! You're small for twelve, are you not?"

I stared at him in astonished exasperation. What did he mean "small"? I was taller than he was, big enough to give a chattering boy a bloody nose, I thought silently—but I merely grunted.

"Where are your parents?" he then asked.

I turned my head away from him so he would not see the tears that stung my eyes. "Both dead," I replied, twisting the tail of my shirt hard in my hands and fighting the urge to weep. I am a player, used to pretending feelings I do not have and hiding those I do. Even so, my throat ached with grief.

Will had all the sensitivity of a tree stump. "How did they die?" he asked eagerly.

I gave my uncle a dark look: *See what you've got me into.* But I said to Will, "Plague." That dread word alone was usually enough to silence anyone.

Not Will, though. "We've had plague in town before. There's a charnel house next to the church crammed floor to ceiling with bones! I often think of the horrible ghosts that must haunt it! Did your parents die in London—?"

At that last question, I had leaped down from the wagon to walk alongside our mare, Molly, with the heart inside me tightening like a hand clutching a hard pebble of pain. If the pest of a boy could not ask me more questions, I would have to tell no more lies. Trust Matthew Bailey, that great laughing hulk of a man, to befriend an annoyance like Will. I was angry to my soul with my big, hearty, broad-faced uncle, so unlike his sister, my mother. She was a frail creature, and though I had claimed her dead of the plague, she was not so. At least I hoped she was not, nor my father, but for all I knew, both of them might have passed on and been buried anytime the past nine months, for I had heard nothing from them in all that time. If they still lived, I thought in despair, they must have forgotten me.

I quickly decided that this Stratford Will was a thick-skull, an ignorant fool. You might have supposed that my jumping down to get away from his flapping tongue would have embarrassed him and stilled his curiosity, but no. Will's jabber rang in my ears as, like Robin Hood launching arrows at a target, the boy loosed question after question at my uncle: What plays did we have by heart? Where would we act? Did we know that two years before, Queen Elizabeth herself had visited Kenilworth Castle, not far from Stratford? That Lord Leicester had produced for the queen a play in which a merman riding on a dolphin sang a song? Did we have fireworks? Those and a hundred other skimble-skamble inquiries barbed the air until at last even Uncle Matthew had his fill and checked young Will's chatter.

"Hold, enough! Your questions pelt me like raindrops; one has not soaked in before another falls!" My uncle's words were angry, but not his tone of voice. Indeed, he fairly chuckled as he spoke to Will, sitting beside him up there in my rightful place.

"I am truly sorry," Will said, though he did not sound sorry at all. "But you have been all over the kingdom! You have played before princes and rogues, you have stood on stages and on cobblestones, you have seen England from one end to the other—"

"And we have heard the chimes at midnight!" interrupted my uncle, laughing. He leaned and called down to me, "Tom, lad, don't be unfriendly, pray. Now be a good fellow and climb back up to sit beside Master Will and try to answer one or two of his questions. 'Tis not far to Stratford, but should I pause to answer Will myself, we would never get to our sleeping-place before we hear those midnight chimes again. Make way, Master Will!"

The wagon creaked to a halt, Dunce and Molly snorted and stamped, and I heard old Ben Fadger swear at the change in motion. Ben perched on a great mound of things, for all we owned, from the lumber for our stage to the tents in which we sometimes slept, the properties and costumes and curtains and all, crammed the wagon to overflowing, and crowning the heap sat crickety, cursing old Ben. No matter how many times Uncle Matthew told him to wait for stillness and steadiness, Ben would always try to stitch up the rips and tears as the wagon wobbled along, and because of that he kept pricking the needle into his horny old fingers. He complained and swore, though no one listened to him much.

As I settled on the seat, Will pointed ahead. "Turn left at the post there, 'tis the nearest way. Did you know we have a fortnight's holiday from school? 'Tis lucky for you, for if you had come this time last week I'd have been hard at the Latin and could not have guided you. Do you really play the women's parts?"

"I do."

"You have a head of hair for it—such soft, golden curls! Do you often fool the audience?"

"I always do," I said.

"Tom's a good actor," put in my uncle. "So are we all, all good actors!"

I knew he was trying to distract Will, but the talkative boy took no notice and gabbled on: "There are but seven of you in all, and plays I have seen often have a dozen or more parts. Do you each take only one part, or do—?"

"Peace, you fast-flowing spring of words!" said my uncle with another easy laugh. "Peace, you hailstorm of questions! By my faith, young Will, you spout words as a whale spouts vapor, blasting them into the air and mystifying the whole neighborhood with the drops. Did you say the mayor's name is Richard Hill?"

Will nearly bounced on the hard seat in his eagerness to answer. "Aye, and a stout friend of my father's, if you need my father's good word. He was bailiff not long ago, and still is on the town council. Oh, I should tell you we don't call the town master the mayor in Stratford, but the bailiff. I—but keep to the other side of the way here, Master Bailey, or else we'll bring down the spite of Speight."

"The spite of spite?" I said, not understanding.

"The man's name is Speight," Will explained with a nervous grin. "Old Edmund Speight. He is a landowner and a miserable miser. These are his fields and, in good faith, I think he thinks the queen's high road is his, too. He—" Will broke off at the sound of raised voices and grimaced. "There he is now," he said, sounding alarmed if not outright frightened. Some distance ahead two men stood, and as we neared I heard them shouting at each other in anger. So full of fury they seemed that I thought they were on the point of striking out with fists—or with blades.

❧ TWO ❧

"Why should wrath be mute,
and fury dumb?"

We drew nearer, and I could see the men stood just beyond a waist-tall hedge that lined the high road. An old man and a young man argued and waved their arms. Their faces shone with sweat and looked much alike, both with hooked noses and long chins, but the elder man's bald head gleamed, pink and bare except for a curling gray fringe round his ears, and the younger wore a cap of tightly curled brown hair, much lighter than young Will's, indeed nearly red in the noontide sun. The two wore good clothing, and I could see at once that these were no poor farmers but substantial men of some fortune.

For all that, they seemed none too happy, and while we were still a fair way from them I heard the young man exclaim peevishly, "Father, you always threaten me with poverty!"

"I mean it this time!" the older man bellowed. "If I leave you none of my land and none of my money, then how will you marry a poor wench? I'll teach you to disobey your father, Francis Speight!"

"Father, how many times have you taken Giles out of your will? How many times have you taken me out? Did you leave everything to me a month ago, when you and my brother quarreled? Now will you give everything to him, after you have more than once sworn he would have nothing? And when you and he fight again, what then will you do—"

" 'Tis a hard thing to have *two* ungrateful sons! A plague on both of you!"

The young man spread his hands. "If you would just be fair, that is all we ask! Father, I'm of age, and Julia—"

"Julia!" The old man fairly spat the word into the younger one's face. "Julia Cabot has no family, no land, nor no fortune, neither! Why would you want to marry such a girl as Julia Cabot?"

"I love her!" the young man returned hotly. By this time we were drawing nigh to them, though I truly think the two were so lost in quarrel that a thunderbolt would scarcely have drawn their attention.

"Love!" the old man snarled, as though love were

something nasty you might scrape off your boot. "I'll have no son of mine dallying with a Cabot wench. Break it off with her now, I say, or else you'll find yourself as poor and landless as she!" The old man turned away and, with a sudden start, he spied us. His mouth jerked down in a frown of quick anger, and his blue eyes glittered in his head. In a handsaw-rasp of a voice, he shouted, "Here, you vagabonds! What mean you, trespassing upon my land? What men are you? Who is that boy there? I've seen him about, the rogue!" He held a stout walking-stick and waved it at us as if it were a sword.

Will shrank down beside me, as if trying to disappear like the Ghost in *The Spaniard's Revenge*, and I saw him make a quick gesture, forehead, breastbone, left shoulder, right shoulder. No one else noticed, because by that time he had all but vanished behind my uncle.

For his part, Uncle Matt had slipped forward on the seat and had swept off his hat, but I noticed he then rested his hand on the rounded head of his own knobbly walking-stick, which was propped beside his right leg. "God give you good day," my uncle said with an air of great courtesy as he reined in Molly and Dunce. "Good sir, we but take the road to Stratford."

"You might have gone straight at the turning and not had to pass through my land! What are you, beggars?"

"No beggars at all. We're Lord Edgewell's Men," my uncle said with a gallant wave of his hand. "The best actors in the world for tragedy, comedy, or—"

"Players! Sinners and rogues, the lot of you! Be off with you, you heathen devils!" the old man snarled. "I'll set the mastiffs on you if you're not clear of my land by the time I reach my house!" He strode away over the hill, leaning on his stick and limping badly but keeping a determined pace.

"And good day to you, too," Uncle Matt said. He shook the reins and both of our horses began to move.

"Father's not in the best of moods today," the young Francis Speight said, falling into place to walk beside the cart. "Hello, Will! What have you been up to, you young rascal?"

Will squirmed. "I was exploring," he said. "I was pretending the Forest of Arden was the New World, and—"

"Not much of a forest," I said, and Will glowered at me. I was right, though. The land had been so cut up by little farms that the only woods left were clumps and straggles. We had not played this part of England before, at least not since I had joined the troupe, but it held few beauties to rouse my admiration.

"But fair fields and flowing streams," young Francis returned. Away from the older mirror image of himself that was his father, Francis Speight was a handsome young fellow, bright of eye and ready with a smile. I did not wonder that he could enchant the heart of a country girl. "I have seen you act before, I think. Were you not in Oxford two years past?"

"Aye, that we were," returned Uncle Matt. "We played, as I recall, *The Soldier's Tragedy* then. Let's see, I acted in that, Alan back there was with us that journey, and Ben Fadger was along, but you wouldn't have seen him, of course. The rest of us are new this trip."

"Especially the young fellow there beside Will," Francis said with a friendly nod to me. "Apprenticed to the theater, are you, lad?"

"To my uncle, and since he is of the theater, to the theater as well, sir," I told him.

"Well, fair be your way into town! If I live, I shall come to see your play!" Francis turned and walked away, taking the same path his father had, as Uncle Matthew clucked to the horses and our wagon trundled onward.

Soon enough we crossed a stout arched stone bridge over the River Avon and rumbled through an open bargate, past a couple of alehouses, one named the Bear and one the Swan, and from there right down the main street and into the heart of town, stopping near a stone cross in the market square. Will squirmed to his feet, ducked past me, and leaped to the ground, running before his soles touched the cobbles. "I'll fetch Bailiff Hill!" he shouted. "I know just where he will be!"

I climbed down more like a Christian than an unmannerly country oaf and led the horses to a trough where they gratefully drank, Dunce occasionally stamping and raising his head to stare about with his oddly stupid expression. Uncle Matthew swaggered over and said, "I thought Molly was favoring this hoof." He stooped and tapped the mare's left front leg, and the gentle horse obediently raised it for him. Pretending to examine it—I knew as well as he that nothing was wrong with her hoof—my uncle murmured to me, "Tom, remember who you are and what you are."

I nodded glumly. "It's just that the boy asked about my parents."

"Mary is my sister as well as your mother. Do you think I am heart-whole and happy, not knowing where she and your father are, not knowing how they fare? But it will never do to let anyone learn of our sorrows or your secret. Remember, there is a price on your father's head, however innocent he is, and that his and your mother's lives hang by the thread of your behavior." He patted Molly's side. "Now tell me who and what you are."

I muttered, "I am Thomas Pryne, apprentice actor. I call you uncle, but you are not my real uncle. My father was Geoffrey Pryne of Gloucestershire, my mother his wife, Eleanor, and they died of plague."

"Good lad," my uncle said loudly. He clapped me on the shoulder and whispered, "Remember that for those who are hunted, all the world is a stage, and the parts they play might just save their lives."

"But why do we have to play in Stratford?" I asked peevishly. We had swung out of our way to come and act in this little, unpromising town.

"I have my reasons," my uncle said, and he turned toward the others.

The four of our company who had tramped a good ten miles since that day's sunrise settled themselves onto a kind of low curb with sighs of contentment. "We had good playing here before," Uncle Matt told them in his cheery voice as he walked over. "One year we were given forty shillings, not to mention the twenty-odd we picked up at collection. The Stratford folk love their plays."

"What will we give them first?" Alan asked, tilting his head to squint up at Uncle Matt. Alan, at twenty, was some six years older than I, clean-shaven like all the other actors. He played the older women, though he was beginning to like strutting about onstage with a sword, acting the part of the young lover or the heroic soldier.

My uncle fell a-musing for a moment and then said, "To prove our worth, we shall first do a mayor's show or, as they call it in Stratford, a bailiff's show, for the city officials and their families. For that, I think something easy and familiar. What say ye to *Youth's Journey*?"

I groaned. That show was a foul old piece of work, a morality play so ancient that it needed to lean on a staff to limp across the stage, and my part in that tottering, threadbare script was that of the Good Angel, which called for a hot, heavy robe with troublesome wings sewn to the shoulders. And to top it off, I would have to wear one of the most uncomfortable wigs.

Sometimes I suspected that my uncle liked the frowsty old play because he acted the part of the Father in it, with one scene of tearful rejoicing that his son had come of age at the beginning, one of tearful lamentation when he thought his son dead near the middle, and one of tearful reunion when his son appeared alive and well at the end. My uncle could weep most convincingly onstage, and he liked to show off that ability.

Watkyn Bishop had his shoe off, shaking from it a tiny chip of rock. He picked the pebble up and exhibited it between thumb and forefinger. "How comes it that a stone as small as a mustard seed feels the size of St. Paul's in your boot? *Youth's Journey*, then? Aye, Master Matt, it suits me well and I'll devil it with the best of them."

Watkyn was a talented comedian, and in this play he acted the role of Vice, a devil whose fiendish plots to snare the soul of Youth ended always with Watkyn himself getting smartly smacked on his head or rump and howling with mock pain, always to roars of laughter from the audience.

The others murmured their satisfaction with the play, except for Ben Fadger, who snorted as he bit short his thread. "Oh, *Youth's Journey*, then. Oh, very good. Just six parts to it, just one part to each player, no work for you at all, oh, no, but me, I have to toil and moil at sewing them blasterd wings onto the angel's robe, and I shall have to let out Youth's hems again, for our Alan will never be done a-growing, no matter how much trouble it is to poor old Ben Fadger, and all them blesserd costumes is at the bottom of the heap, too, so here's old wore-out Ben a-having to stay up to the morning hours a-mending and a-airing of them, small thanks do I get for it."

"Thank you, Ben," said my uncle, raising his knobbly walking-stick in a graceful salute. "Thank you, thank you, and a thousand times thank you."

"Thank-yous ain't pennies," growled Ben, still unmollified. "Which I wish they was, and all in my breeches-pocket, and my breeches in an alehouse, and me inside my breeches."

"And all the ale inside of you, you old rogue of a natomy," said Peter Stonecypher with a chuckle. He would play Parson Wise. After Ben, Peter was the next eldest among us, well above forty, a doddering old man, as far as strolling players went, for the life on the road was not kind to elderly bones.

Michael Moresby, a young man so slender you might well have mistaken him, too, for an anatomy or skeleton, was pacing back and forth on his long, bony grasshopper legs while he muttered to himself, and I knew he was remembering his lines as Death in the play. Poor Michael was always frightened of forgetting his part, and ever and always swore that before he stepped onto any stage his mind went utterly blank. Somehow, though, he found the words, or the words found him, and in roles of trembling old men or weird grotesques he had no equal. In his hollow Death's voice, he boomed, "I am come to bring ye doom! Be ye never so blithe, ye will never more thrive, for with my scythe will I shear your life-thread ye hold ever so dear!"

I shivered, seeing in my mind's eye Michael dressed in his black Death's robe, his face whitened with makeup, with dark eye sockets painted in, and his nose seeming a gaping triangular void, and teeth painted onto his lips to make a perfect image of a skull. Michael himself might be afraid of forgetting his lines, but when he bestrode the stage as grinning, spindle-shanked Death, the Grim Reaper, the audience was always afraid of Michael.

"A sail! A sail!" shouted Alan, waving his cap in the air. "Behold a ship of a hundred-odd ton, towed by a rowboat!"

I guessed that the solid and substantial man following the running Will toward us was Richard Hill, the bailiff of Stratford town. My uncle gave all of us players a meaningful jerk of his head, and we lined up before our wagon, making a company bow as the man drew near.

"Here they are!" Will was panting. "See, Bailiff Hill, I told you they were elegant players!"

The large man was huffing and puffing, but his ruddy face split into a smile that showed he was missing a tooth here and there. "So you did, young William. God give you good day, my excellent players. Whose men are you?"

My uncle expanded like the proud frog in the fable and, gesturing broadly, he replied in a hearty, carrying voice that turned heads and drew onlookers as honey draws flies: "With submission, my good sir, we are Lord Edgewell's Men, and the best actors in the world for tragedy, comedy, pastoral, interlude, and morality! We can give you a song, dance upon a rope, freeze your blood with horror, melt it again with romance, split your sides with laughter, and break your heart with tragedy." From inside his doublet he produced our papers and with a flourish handed them over to the smiling Bailiff Hill.

Some of the townsmen applauded this fustian speech, but I simply rolled my eyes. I had heard it dozens of times, and indeed little did my uncle Matthew ever say that he had not already thought of and rehearsed in private. None of them knew or could suspect how serious a man he could be, or how valiant in defending a family under a sentence of death, as my poor father and mother were.

As for Will, his brown eyes shone as if he owned us and were proud of us for making such a good appearance. He absorbed every word my uncle spoke, and I could see that each one went straight to his soul. He might be nothing more than a rude country boy, but already I could tell he loved his books and his tales and words, words, words. Still, I judged him book-wise and world-ignorant, though I felt quite sure that my uncle would tell me the boy had no harm in him at all.

But already I was beginning to hate him.

❧ Three ❧

"Murder most foul . . ."

By afternoon everything had been settled. Sometimes when we had funds and it was lawful, we slept in country inns, my uncle and I in one room, everyone else in another. At present we had little money, so we were not to stay within the town at all, but would camp on some ground south of the town boundary, not far from the river. That was no great hardship, for people in many places disliked us, looking upon a strolling player as no more respectable than a beggar and no more to be trusted than a thief. We were used to living rough and sleeping outside the town limits.

We set up our three tents and had a quick meal of bread, cheese, and small ale—too small for the other, older players, who complained of its weakness. Then the grown-ups all went to the Guild Hall, carrying carpenter's tools, for they would hurriedly knock together the stage on which we would act for the town's masters and, perhaps later, for the wealthier inhabitants, before we moved back outside to the market square for our last performances. Only Ben was left at the camp, cursing and sewing for all he was worth, and merely to get away from his eternal grumbling, I suffered Will's company as he showed me the very limited sights of Stratford.

The place was just another country market town, with cobbled streets and half-timbered houses. It was well enough in its way, I supposed, but if God had picked the whole place up and dropped it into the middle of London, it would have been utterly swallowed. By the time Will showed me the Guild Hall, our men had already put up the low stage and were working on its temporary ceiling, since one of the great effects of *Youth's Journey* was the Angel's flight down to earth, and I had to fly down from somewhere. At the rate they were hammering, they would be done within an hour, and then I knew most of them would be off to one of the taverns to quench their thirst.

On the floor above the long meeting room was Will's school. It was empty but unlocked, and we went inside for a peep at the rows of ink-stained forms and benches where

Will said he and his classmates sat and translated Latin into English and vice versa.

Then we left the sound of pounding hammers behind us as we wandered back toward the bridge and passed the Swan tavern, from which drifted the yeasty fragrances of ale and fresh bread, and from there we roamed up one street and down another, with him talking, talking, talking the whole time, boasting of Stratford's glories, finishing with a description of its beautiful church.

When he showed it to me, I had to agree that, though small, the house of worship was a handsome one. Trinity Church lifted its white steeple above a pretty spread of ground down near the river, and around it lay a green churchyard bristling with crumbling gray gravestones. The charnel house stood to one side of the church itself, a bleak stone building with no windows and a great heavy door. A gray-haired man spotted us as Will was describing the contents and came bounding over toward us, shouting hoarsely, "I'll leave ye inside this time, ye pest!"

"Run!" Will shouted in alarm.

"Who's that man?" I yelped, but Will was already fleeing, and he legged it away with all his speed as I pelted close behind. The wiry man hopped along behind us, sweeping his arms through the air like a windmill and laughing wildly, as though his wits were quite astray, and he left off only when we were a hundred yards clear of the churchyard. We ran along the riverbank, while behind us the man danced in place, shaking both fists in the air and sending curses after us that fairly turned the air blue. We sped past the plot of land where our tents stood before stopping to catch our breath, stooped over with our hands on our knees, and I gasped, "Who—who was that mad fellow?"

"Sexton," Will panted. He breathed hard for some moments, and then added, "Costard, they call him. Real name, Clarence Coste. Believe me or not, but Costard was a learned man once, a clerk of a church, before he took hard to drink. He disgraced himself somehow, but nobody will tell me what he did. Now he's glad enough to have the cleaning of the church and the burying of the dead to do." He panted a little more, leaned close to me, and added in a low voice, "He did something terrible to me once."

"What?" I asked, having wind for little more than the one word.

Will shook his head. "It's too awful to talk about."

After catching my breath, I said, "The people of your town hold no friendliness inside them. This raving sexton. That angry old man."

Will shrugged. "They are not the whole town. Costard's

wits are drowned with drink, and Speight is possessed with a devil of hate."

"Toward actors," I said.

"Toward everyone," returned Will. "But most especially toward his own twin sons."

"Francis Speight's brother is his twin?"

"Aye. Giles and Francis, and they look very like each other. But Francis is much the friendlier. He taught me how to fish—come on, and I'll show you where I fish!"

We passed a mill and crossed a narrow footbridge over the Avon and for another three or four hours we rambled, roaming until the sun had sunk low. Will had led me a fine walk, far down the Avon, and we trudged back toward town with less spirit than we had set out. Purple twilight had fallen when we crossed the arched stone bridge that led to town, where candlelight already gleamed yellow in all the windows, and I began to feel just how hungry I was after my half-day's roaming. Will paused on the bridge, rested his arms on the stone rail, and hung his head over, staring down at the dark water flowing and splashing below us. "Listen," he said. "Do rivers sing to you?"

"What?" I asked him.

"You know, do you hear the water and let the sound make words in your head? Listen now to the Avon: 'flowing onward, flowing onward, flowing onward to the sea. What is this now, what is this now, what is this to hinder me?' Can't you just hear it saying that?"

"I hear it saying 'gurgle gurgle gurgle,'" I returned waspishly.

"Listen with the ear of your mind," Will said. "Let it sing! Everything has a voice, Tom. The wind, the birds in the trees, the crickets playing their violas in the tall grass. What's wrong with you?"

"Nothing," I said sharply. I had started at the word "viola," but, thankfully, Will hadn't seemed to notice. "To me, the river sounds like a river, that's all."

Will sighed. "The Avon sounds to me as if it speaks of travels and wonders."

"It sounds to me as if a log has caught on one of the pillars."

Suddenly Will put both hands beside his face, making a sort of tunnel round his eyes, and stared down at the water as if he saw his own salvation floating there on the river's troubled surface.

I asked, "What's the matter with you?"

At the same instant, Will asked, "What's that white thing?"

I looked down too, and in the darkness could see only

the white traces of froth on the water's surface, swirling in little whirlpools. I said as much.

"Not that," Will said impatiently. "There, see? It's almost under you. No, not straight downward. More to your left."

And then I did glimpse what he was pointing at, a blur of white wavering in the gloom, glimmering as water flowed over it, sometimes hiding it entirely, sometimes leaving it to shine faintly in the dark air: something caught against the foot of one of the bridge arches and pinned there by the rushing water. "I can't tell what it is," I said. "Maybe a white log or something."

"A mystery! Come on." Will scrambled off the bridge and down the bank, and all unwillingly I followed, ducking under the dank-smelling arch of the bridge, hoping not to blunder into the river and drown. Will had picked up a fallen branch and was prodding something with it. "Here it is. What is it?"

"Why ask me?" I demanded of this irritating boy. "I can see no more than you—"

"I've snagged it! Now if I can just tow it in and not lose it to the water—grab hold, Tom, and help me."

I reached out in the dark and my hand closed around the cold, wet, rough bark of the limb. Will and I leaned back, and whatever it was peeled away from the bridge footing and curved toward us, the branch hooked into it.

My stomach fluttered then, at the strange movement of the thing, the looseness of it. A drowned sheep, maybe, and I braced myself in case it was a rotten one, stinking with decay.

Will cried out, a wordless astonishment. "Help me pull him up!" he said.

"Him?"

Stooping, I felt my blood cold in my veins. The shape was a man. Will grasped his left arm and tried to haul him up onto the riverbank. The bald head, thrown back, trailed gray, wispy straggles of hair. The slack mouth hung open, a black gap in the pale blur of face, and the eyes seemed to be open too.

Even in the darkness I knew that terrible face, for I had seen it earlier that day as it writhed in anger.

It was the face of old Farmer Speight, and he was dead, dead as Doomsday.

❧ Four ❧

"... some sufficient honest witnesses."

"How did you boys find him?"

It was half an hour later, and in the darkening night a small crowd stood at the foot of the Stratford bridge, half of them bearing lanterns. One of them was a constable of the place, a thickset man named Taylor, wearing a buff leather jerkin. I thought from the tone of his voice he was a bit thick in the head as well as in midriff.

"We heard the water!" Will exclaimed, so impatient that he practically danced from side to side. "Ask Tom. It sounded as if something had caught under the bridge, he said, so we went down to see and I found a tree branch and hooked it into his shirt—see where the tear is there—and we pulled him to shore."

"And then we ran to fetch you," I said, feeling a dull fear that lingered from the shock we'd had. I did not like these strangers staring at me and I wondered where my uncle was.

"Sure, old Edmund must have been taken sick and fallen in," someone in the crowd murmured.

"Taken drunk, you mean," someone else scoffed.

"Nay, I've never seen him drunk," another offered. "He was too close with a penny to spend it on a drop of wine or ale."

"He was in the Swan this evening, though," another man said. "I saw him come in as I was leaving, and that was some time before sunset."

"Has anyone been sent to fetch his sons?" a woman asked. "They ought to know, poor lads."

Constable Taylor growled, "All that's attended to, Mistress Quickly. Where is Dr. Wells?"

A jeering, rough voice cut in: "He needs no doctor, not old Speight, nor never will again, I warrant. He needs a grave digger, and good Costard's just at hand, as the pickpocket said."

Will started, and so did I, for the hoarse voice was that of Clarence Coste, the mad sexton who had driven us from Trinity churchyard a few hours earlier. The gray-haired madman stood in the glare of the constable's lantern, leering down at the dead and dripping body. "Dead and gone, dead and gone, and his body's cold as stone," he crooned, as though he were singing a dirge for the old man.

"Much you care," Taylor said irritably. "It's a few pennies in your pocket, isn't it?"

Coste smiled down at the body, as if he saw it as a pile of coins, not a poor drowned fellow Christian. "Aye, I'll have the digging of his grave to attend to. I'll dig this one deep, to put him down closer to his eternal home, for such as Speight couldn't hope to rise to heaven. Them's good clothes he has on, though, and I reckon the rip in the shirt might be mended. Wonder if we're of a size."

"Costard, please!" one of the women said.

He gave her an exaggerated bow. "Sorry, my lady. But 'tis true that in any town there are two men who always have the largest wardrobes: the hangman and the grave digger!"

The crowd on the bridge was growing every minute as more people saw the lanterns and came out to learn what was afoot. A learned-looking man pushed through the crowd. "What's this, Taylor?" he asked the constable, his voice sounding weary. "Why am I sent for?"

"Dr. Wells," replied Constable Taylor, "tell me, is there life in that man?"

The physician then saw the body for the first time and knelt beside it. He touched the cold throat. "Life? Not a sign of it. This man is dead," he said.

"Dead and gone," crooned Coste, and people around him shushed him.

"Drownded?" asked the constable.

"I think not," the doctor muttered, his long fingers moving as busily as a spinning spider as he felt the old man's skull. He held up his hand, and in the yellow lantern light I could see a watery, brownish-red liquid that slowly dripped from his fingers. "He has a bad lump on the back of his head, and I can feel the bone of his skull moving beneath the press of my fingers. Someone struck him hard, hard enough to knock the life from him, and threw his body into the water after he was dead."

"Murder, you mean?" the constable asked.

"I would say so. I don't see how Speight could have knocked himself on the back of the head if he simply fell in. I think someone wanted him dead and hit him with something really hard, a stone, a heavy stick, or something like that, to kill him."

The crowd buzzed with people repeating the doctor's words: "Murder!" "Struck on the mazzard!" "Someone killed him!"

The doctor absently wiped his bloody fingers on Speight's wet clothes. "Very curious, this."

"What do you mean?" the constable asked.

The doctor looked up, squinting into the lantern light. "Why, just this: In the Swan, not one good hour ago, old Speight here asked me and John Shakespeare to bear witness to his signature, and so we did, signing and sealing so that all was legal."

"A deed?" the constable asked.

"No, not a deed," the doctor said, getting up with a grunt. "No, we witnessed Edmund Speight's signature on a piece of paper that he said was his last will and testament."

"Murder!" Coste said, though he sounded quite pleased. He raised his hoarse old voice and sang out in the night:

"The moon saw it done, and the bat and the owl:
In the dead of the night, 'twas murder most foul."

Someone grabbed my sleeve, making me jump. But it was only Will. He whispered in my ear, "Come! We must find my father!"

He fairly dragged me away from the bridge and the crowd, toward the Swan tavern. "Why do we have to find your father?" I gasped. I had rather find my uncle, for the death of the old man had left me feeling strangely uneasy, and I wanted him to speak words of comfort to me, as he often had done.

"Because my father is John Shakespeare, and he put his name to the will!" he told me. "You heard the doctor—he and my father were the witnesses. Come on. If we can find what was in the will, I'll give you any odds we can put our hands on the murderer!"

"You think one of Speight's sons killed him?" I asked.

"It's plain!" Will said. "And the two of us, you and I, can resolve the mystery and so win the applause of the whole town! Come, come, let's question my father!"

"Are you daft?" I asked. "No! I'll do no such thing."

In the darkness I could tell that Will darted a quick look back toward the crowd on the bridge. He leaned close to me and in an urgent voice he said, "Yes, you will! You have to!"

"I do not!"

"You do, or else"—he lowered his voice to a whisper—"or else I'll tell them all the truth about you."

"And what truth is that?" I asked with scorn.

In the same low voice he said, "That you are a girl, Tom Pryne."

I felt cold again. He had me there.

∝ Five ∞

"Men should be what they seem . . ."

I stayed frozen for scarcely two beats of my alarmed heart. Then I seized Master Will by his jerkin and dragged him into a dark corner, an angle of a building, and thrust him so hard against the wall his head bounced back and the teeth clicked in his mouth. In a voice of rage I told the young fool, "You are not to say that!"

Until that instant I had not realized how much taller than Will I was. As I gripped his jerkin with both my hands, both of his clutched at my wrists. "Let me go! Put me down!"

I shook him again, drumming his head on the wall behind him. "I mean it, Will! You are not to tell anyone that you suppose I'm a girl! Promise me that you will not, or I *will* hurt you!" I hauled at his jerkin.

Despite the fact that I had lifted him so his toes dangled clear off the ground—he did not weigh nearly so much as I—Will laughed at that. " 'Suppose?' " he gasped. "There is no 'suppose' about it, or else it is but a counterfeit 'suppose.' Do you think I am blind and deaf, forsooth? In good faith, I knew you for a girl as soon as I saw you—I knew you as well as he that fathered you!"

"Then why did you say nothing!"

His voice fell to a contrite level: "I believe that a person's secrets are secret for a reason, that's why. I thought that when the time came that you wanted me to know, you would tell me. Is that good enough, Tom? What is your real name?"

I let him down. "You can still call me 'Tom.' You will tell no one," I insisted. "Or else I—I will tell them all you are a Catholic!"

He stood breathing in the dark for a short spell, sounding as if he had run a quarter-mile. "You saw me cross myself when old Speight surprised us."

"I did."

He tried to laugh. He did not sound so sure of himself, and the laugh rang weak and false in my ears. "Go ahead and tell if you want. That is no news to folk hereabout. My mother was an Arden, and in the whole shire they are one of the best-known families to follow the old religion. People know what we are, and they are willing to overlook us."

"There are those elsewhere who would not overlook you, though," I said. "The queen's men would surely not—should I drop a word in the right place!" My voice was trembling. I heard tears rising in it, but could not fight them down. They broke out in a sob and when it had passed, I said vengefully, "I hate all Catholics!"

"*Shh!*" Will awkwardly patted my shoulder, but I jerked away from him. "Say not so! Shall I tell you a great secret? My schoolmaster is a Catholic! There are many in Stratford and round about. We—I mean, *they*—are not so bad. Why should you hate them?"

I felt my face burning so hot with shame and fury that it seemed to me it should glow of its own light, like an ember in the dark. "Because my mother and father helped a condemned priest out of the country. He was a man whom my father had known from boyhood, and out of mere friendship they helped him board a ship for France and safety, and for that act of simple kindness they have been named outlaws and have gone into hiding," I said, trying to keep my voice low. "And now I know not whether they live or are dead. I've not seen them in the better part of a year! And because the queen's men might seize upon me and torture me to bring them out of hiding,

I've been forced to this wretched pretense—to make believe that I am a boy and act onstage with my uncle. It's a miserable life, being afraid for myself, afraid for my uncle, and afraid for my parents!"

Then I could not help weeping. Will kept murmuring, "Don't cry, don't. It's all right, really it is. I won't tell. Please don't cry anymore." He tried to give my shoulder more of his awkward, well-meaning pats, but I swatted his hand away.

"Stop it," I said, slowly regaining command of my feelings. *Save it for the stage,* my uncle would have told me. There you need to call on tears and rage; keep them inside during the hours you are not acting, and save such feelings for the stage. Easy advice to give, I thought, and hard advice to follow.

"Come," said Will. "I shall swear to keep your secret, you mine. Agreed?"

Finally swallowing hard and forcing down the great aching lump in my throat, I said, "Yes."

"Let us go, then," Will said urgently. "We have to find my father, and quickly. You and I may be able to use our wits and settle this matter of murder! If we can but discover the murderer, why, think of the glory! Think of the praise! It will be better than treading any stage, I'll warrant you. Come away, and come quickly!"

Hastily rubbing my eyes on my sleeve, I followed him to the sign of the Swan. Inside we found a roar of drunken voices, laughing, cursing, talking. The air hung heavy with the aroma of beer and ale, and smoke from the candles had darkened the beams and ceiling in the course of many evenings such as this one. It was clear to me that the news of Speight's death had not yet found the legs to run here, for not a soul seemed to be speaking of it. Will looked around and led me to a corner where a heavy, red-faced man sat, hoisting a mug of ale and laughing uproariously at something just said by his neighbor, a skinny fellow whose face was all nose, his round head crowned with a bristly growth of hair like yellow straw.

"Why, Will!" the red-faced man said in a booming, amiable voice as we drew nigh. "What, is it so late by the clock that your mother has sent you here to fetch me? It cannot be. I swear, it has been not much more than a minute since I sat to drink!"

"Father," Will said in a low and urgent voice, "I must speak with you, and not in this place."

His father stared hard at him with piercing eyes. "I see. Then let me but finish this ale, for it is too good to waste." He raised his tankard, which still held a goodly amount, and began to drink it down rapidly.

The straw-haired man laughed. "He's a one for his ale, is

good John Shakespeare! Lads, did you ever see the hot sun kiss a dish of butter and make it melt? He compounds that! His sunny red face makes ale turn to vapor!"

John Shakespeare pounded his empty tankard on the table. "Aye, and now you shall make your coppers turn into ale, for 'tis your turn to pay for the round, Master Fitch! So do you attend to that bit of sorcery, and I'll attend to my boy here. Come, Will."

We followed him out of the Swan. Will's father had taken so much ale that his gait was a little tottery, and he weaved as he walked, more than once putting a hand on a chair back or on the wall to steady his step. Once outside in the cooler air, he snorted in three great long breaths and then muttered, "Now what's ado, Will?"

In hurried, hushed tones, Will told him everything— about the way we had found Edmund Speight's dead body beneath the bridge, and about what the doctor had said concerning the way the old man had met his death. With his head somewhat fuddled with drink, John Shakespeare seemed to take a long time to understand it all, but at last he exclaimed, "What! Dead and tossed in the water? By my faith, that bears a frosty sound. Murder in Stratford! Will, you go home to your mother. I'll to the bridge and tell them what I know."

"What do you know, Father?" Will demanded.

In the dim yellow light spilling out from the tavern window, John Shakespeare passed a broad hand over his great pink ham of a face. "Why, I know that Edmund Speight came into the tavern angry, for that he had searched all about town for Lawyer Collins, and had not found him anywhere. Nor was Mr. Collins in the tavern, for as someone told Speight, he has gone to Oxford for the week. You know Edmund and his foul temper. He fell to cursing like a very drab, swearing so that he all but broke the peace. He even quarreled with the leader of the players who came to town today, with that Matthew Bailey. Then he asked two of us to witness his signature upon a folded sheet of paper, and the tavern wench found us pen and ink, and witness we did, Dr. Wells and I."

"What was written on the paper?" asked Will.

"Will, you know that I can read broad print after a fashion, but handwriting is too hard for me. But 'twas no need at all to read, for Speight had folded the papers so no words showed. All he asked me to do was watch him sign his name, then make my mark that I had witnessed him do it. Dr. Wells did the same."

"It must have been his will," I said. "We heard him threaten to change it this afternoon, and the doctor said he told him that's what it was. He wanted you to witness his new will. Pray tell me what he said to Matthew Bailey, for he's my uncle."

John Shakespeare grunted. "Pray don't take it to heart, but old Speight denounced your uncle as a harlotry beggarly trespasser, a very vagabond, a worthless fellow of no mark nor likelihood in the world, and warned him that the next time he passed close to Speight's farm, he would find hounds set loose on his heels. I'll say this for thy uncle, lad: He is a fellow of mettle and did not care to be so threatened, and he spoke back to old Speight. The two of them had hot words and both stormed out angry, first your uncle, later Speight. That is all."

I felt sick. If my uncle and Edmund Speight had left the tavern after arguing so loudly, less than an hour before Speight had turned up dead—

"Come," Will said to me, and we followed his father the few yards down to the bridge. The crowd had grown so large that I thought all of Stratford, all two thousand-odd souls in the place, had gathered there above the forlorn and sodden body of the dead man.

"What's ado here, Constable Taylor?" John Shakespeare bawled out.

"Here he is!" some of them said, and they closed in a knot around him and fell to gabbling about the dead body. From the way they spoke, the people of the town clearly regarded Will's father as a man of some judgment and importance. As he listened to three people at once, John Shakespeare caught sight of Will and me standing a few steps off in the light of the lanterns, and in a firm voice he ordered us away.

"Come on, Tom," Will said to me. "I'll find out tonight when the crowner will sit on the case—"

"The what?" I asked.

"The crowner," Will repeated impatiently. "The man who decides if a death is murder or not. Have you never heard the word?"

"I've heard of a coroner," I told him. I had never heard that country way of pronouncing it before, but in Stratford I would soon get used to it.

"However you say it, the crowner will sit on the case, and I'll contrive some way for us to be there and learn what he says. Right now 'tis best to leave, for Father will be all in a rage should we remain against his orders. First I'll take you to your people's tents, and then I'll go home. My mother will be worried."

We went along a cobbled street—Henley Street, Will told me—and he pointed out his house, which had a little leather shop on the right side, reeking with the odors of tanned calf and sheepskins. "My father's business," Will explained. "I'm supposed to help him on my holidays from school, but in June few wealthy folk want gloves and the like, and so he buys and sells a few things and does not much mind if I'm not in the shop every day. This way."

A half-mile or so along I saw the low glowing campfire near the tents and wagon, and in a moment we had come up to the tent I shared with my uncle. "I'll be here betimes," Will whispered. "Not a word of our secrets, mind! Tomorrow we shall learn what's what."

He melted away in the darkness. I could hear the harsh rumbles of my uncle's snoring. For one wild moment I wanted to wake him and warn him, to urge him to stir the actors up, stow the wagon, and put miles between us and Stratford. Still, I knew my uncle. Never in my wildest fancies could I see this gentle man as bearing the guilt of any contrived murder.

And so I crept into the tent, found my sleeping pallet, and lay down. I did not expect to sleep a wink that long night, and indeed I slept very little. In the morning, I thought, I would have to tell them of the death of Edmund Speight. Sometime very late I finally did slip into slumber, and the dreams that came were horrible, with a man rising up from the depths of dark water, his dead eyes glaring, to clutch at my legs and drag me down.

On the whole I would rather have remained awake.

∞ Six ∞

"Go thou and seek the crowner,
and let him sit . . ."

Early the next morning, so early that it was still dark, something *did* grab my ankle and shake it. I woke with a gasp and heard Will's whisper: "Not a word!"

I wormed out of my bedding and, shoes in hand, ducked out of the tent. "What time is it?" I asked.

"Before the first cock-crow," Will whispered back. "Come on. There will be no need for you today— the crowner's been sent for, and the town won't permit you to practice your play with such serious business afoot."

Realizing it would be of small use to protest, I said, "All right, then," and began to put on my shoes.

As Will waited impatiently, I made myself ready, and

then I followed him back into Stratford. Outside his house, he said, "You wait here!"

I stood lurking in the shadows, and in a few moments he popped out again. "Come!"

He led me to the Guild Hall. "We'll have to hide before the first of them come in," Will told me. "I have a good place. First, though, are you hungry?"

"As the ravening lion in *The Tragedy of Pyramus*," I answered, for I had eaten nothing since the afternoon of the previous day.

"Here, hold out your hands."

I felt something—two somethings—round and hard and still lingeringly warm drop into my palms: boiled eggs. And then a nice piece of bread, slippery with butter. "I've a bottle of water, too," Will told me. "I've had breakfast already. Eat and we'll go hide."

I bowed my head and murmured a short prayer.

"What? This is no occasion to pray," Will said. "We don't have much time!"

"My mother taught me to make grace the prologue to every meal, even if it be only an egg and butter," I snapped back, "and so I will give thanks to God." I cracked the eggs and ate them, one after the other, without salt but with hearty appetite. The bread was delicious, yeasty-sweet and rich with butter. "I thank you, too," I said grudgingly when I had finished it and had taken a long drink from the bottle.

"Now, if you need to—to go to the privy," Will stammered, "you had better do it. We're likely to be hid for hours, and a full bladder will make you miserable."

"Don't follow me." I found a private place and made myself comfortable, then felt my way back to where Will waited. "All right. If we are to do this clay-brained thing, let's begin it."

By then we heard cocks crowing all around, and the sky had begun to lighten. Will took me into the Guild Hall's great room. In the darkness at the far end our temporary stage waited. We stepped up onto the platform, under the low ceiling, supported on either side by a kind of frame that gave actors waiting their turn a place to stand hidden from the audience. Just off center above us yawned the dark rectangle of the open trapdoor through which I would make my entrance, dangling on a rope that ran across through pulleys, so the free end could be held by my uncle, standing behind the stage-right frame.

Will asked me to lock my hands and give him a lift so he could grasp the edge of the opening. Kicking and grunting, he hauled himself up into the cramped, narrow space. Reaching an arm down, he said, "Now you!"

Climbing was harder than it looked. I made much ado to hoist myself up and worm through the opening. Even lying flat on my stomach, I felt the press of a rafter in the small of my back. The little space was only inches deep, and not meant to hold great weight. I hoped we would not both come tumbling down in a shower of boards.

Maybe it would all hold as long as Will and I were separate, lying flat with one of us on each side of the angel's open trapdoor. We could peek down through cracks between the planks and see on the stage itself the scarred wooden table where the coroner would hold court. We could raise our heads—but not too much, or we would bump them—to get a glimpse of the benches where the citizens would sit to listen.

"Now," Will said, "here we are set."

"Wait," I said, trying to get my breath back. "Why did you climb up that way? If you'd asked, I could have told you that there's a kind of ladder built in to the back of the frame. Why didn't we take that easy path?"

"Why, what sport would that have been?" he asked, sounding astonished, adding "Ouch!" a moment later as I hit him hard on the shoulder.

To beguile away the time, he had me tell him about plays

I had been in, and he drank in the tales like one dying of thirst. I recited to him the opening lines I had in *Youth's Journey*:

> *"O give us heed, good people all,*
> *And with patience list unto our play:*
> *We tell of how young men may fall,*
> *And how life's span is but a day.*
> *Will Youth o'ercome his tempters strong?*
> *Or else to pain shall he be ta'en?*
> *Lend ears, lend eyes, and then ere long*
> *His life's journey we will show plain."*

"Brave show! Rare words!" Will exclaimed in delight.

"You'd want them to be rare if you had to say them as you dangled from a rope around your middle," I muttered, flicking the pulley attached to the rafter so it jingled. He had me go through all my speeches, and after but one recital, I truly believe he had them as much by heart as I did, without the struggle and bother of trying to memorize them.

In return, he told me of his schoolwork. That year he and his classmates had done a translation of some old Roman play by Plautus. He could not stop giggling as he told me about it: a farce in which a set of twins who had been separated soon after birth, now grown and each one not known to the other, got into scrape after scrape, each twin always being taken for his unknown brother. I did not think much of it, for mistaken identity is an old tired device, but Will kept muttering lines he had translated, laughing immoderately as he did.

And then two yawning men came into the room and busied themselves with preparations. Now that it was full morning, I could sneak a look down through the cracks in the planks below me to watch the two men spread the table set upon the stage with a blue velvet cover, worn but rich-looking. It would have done for a royal robe had Ben Fadger the chance to work on it with his needle and scissors. A smaller table placed off to the side, Will told me, was where the scribe would sit to take down all that would be said during the inquest.

"Shh!" Will shushed me without need as men began to come in, men whose clothes proclaimed them to be sober, steady citizens. A lean, pale fellow wearing a starched white collar the size of a dinner platter entered, head down, speaking in low tones to Constable Taylor. This must have been the coroner: a grave, older man with long white hair and a short, pointed white beard. He settled himself in the chair behind the table and then conferred in a low voice with another man who sat at the smaller table, armed with paper, pen, and ink.

Will nudged me and I looked up and caught my breath. Two identical men had come in, side by side. One surely was Francis Speight, the son of the dead man to whom my uncle had spoken on the way into Stratford—but which one? They were like mirror images of each other and indeed were even dressed alike, both of them in somber black and silver. "The brother?" I whispered.

"Aye," said Will. "Giles Speight, in his temper more like his father than his twin, for all they resemble each other!"

"Which is he?" I asked.

"Watch and you will see."

The two of them came forward, beckoned by one of the men of Stratford, and sat side by side on a bench near the front. The one on the left crossed his arms and sank his chin on his breast, a frown tugging down the corners of his mouth. The other waved at several people and accepted their condolences with a sad smile. "Francis is on the right," I said.

"Yes," Will agreed. "Giles is sour, like his father."

I was no longer staring at the twin sons of Edmund Speight, but at my uncle, who had that moment come in. He stood just inside the doorway, sweeping the room with his gaze, and he looked so worried that it was all I could do not to call out to him. Behind him some little stir broke out, and I saw Bishop and Stonecypher being pushed back by men bearing staves. My uncle said something to them, and the two members of our troupe unwillingly turned away. They were not to be admitted to the hearing, it seemed, but I supposed my uncle was a witness and so privileged to mingle with the gentlemen of Warwickshire.

The proceedings began with lines as rehearsed as any in one of our plays, spoken in a singsong that made them seem trivial and unimportant. Her Gracious Majesty's name was mentioned (how gracious, I wondered resentfully, was a queen who would hound her subjects as my poor parents had been worried and hounded?), and then the coroner, in a reedy, high voice, read from a notebook, telling us all that we were there to witness a coroner's inquest into the cause of death of Edmund Speight, Esquire, late of this parish.

The first to speak was Constable Taylor, and after he was sworn in, his tale came out in clotted bits and jumbled pieces. He mentioned only that he had been told by certain "youths" that something resembling a body was beneath the bridge. He told of summoning the doctor—but then had to go back and explain that *first* he had gone to the bridge and had made sure that the body was a body, and that it was dead. "If you knew the man was dead," the coroner asked in a testy voice, "why did you send for the doctor? Did you hope he would get better?"

"No, m'lord," Taylor said, his beefy face wrinkled in an effort to think. "But Dr. Wells would know more about a dead 'un than I did, and so I thought he might tell us if Master Edmund had died through accident, or sudden illness, or if he had been murdered, or mayhap had done himself a mischief."

"Us?" asked the coroner. "What do you mean 'us'? Who else was there, Constable?"

"Everyone," Taylor said helplessly. "Not all at once, but they came a bit at a time, in ones and twos like. Anyway, Dr. Wells came, and he examined the body, and told us it was his opinion—"

"That is enough," said the coroner. "Thank you, Constable Taylor. Dr. Wells, would you come forward to testify, please?"

The doctor took Taylor's place, swore to tell the truth and, crisply, with little in the way of flourishes or learned speech, told how he had felt the man's skull, had found a broken bone and a great lump, and had concluded that Edmund Speight had been hit before falling into the water.

At that point one of the jurors asked, "Could he not have struck his head on the stonework of the bridge as he fell?"

Dr. Wells considered. "I cannot say that is absolutely impossible," he conceded. "However, to me it looked much like the kind of blow a man would give another with a staff or stick. It was awkwardly placed to have been an accidental injury, but just the kind of wound that might have been made by a man striking hard and downward at the back of Speight's head."

Then the doctor told of having been in the tavern earlier and having been approached by Edmund Speight, who carried papers that evidently had been heavily written on but that he kept folded so the writing could not be seen. "He told me it was his will," the doctor said, "and that, lacking his lawyer, he needed two witnesses. I looked round and saw John Shakespeare, who knew Speight as well as I did, and so I took Speight to John's table and we witnessed his signature." Will's father took the stand for just a few moments then, to tell the same story and to mention that Speight had been in bad humor and had railed at my uncle when he first came into the tavern.

And then they called my uncle. He lumbered to the front of the room, looking so apprehensive that I felt a strong pang of sorrow for him. He swore to tell the truth, and then told his name and gave his London lodgings, in Cheapside, as his address. He explained that we were strolling players come to Stratford to give a show and to make a few coppers; and then the coroner asked him about Speight. Taking a deep breath, my uncle said, "As we rode toward Stratford yesterday, we chanced to take the way that leads past his farm. He stopped us with a threat and accused us of trespassing—but we never left the queen's high road, upon my soul!"

He went on to explain that, the previous night, he had been refreshing himself in the tavern when Speight saw him and came over to rant insults. "He called us all thieves and beggars," my uncle recalled, "and ordered us not to depart the same way we came, or else he would set his dogs upon us."

"And how did you answer?" demanded the coroner.

My uncle's face grew scarlet. "I told him what I have told you, sir. I said that we were on the high road, not on his land at all; and I will confess with shame that I made some intemperate remarks about old men who thought they owned the world. He did not welcome my speech."

"No," someone said. "Edmund wouldn't have."

A ripple of laughter ran round the room, and the Speight twin on the left—Giles—leaped to his feet, balled his fists, and glared round the room until one of the servants begged him to be seated again. The coroner then asked, "And when you and Speight left, did you go out together?"

"No, we did not," my uncle said very definitely. "I finished the beer I was drinking and left before him. From the tavern I walked through the town and so to our camp."

"And did you see him?"

"I did not, nor did I look for him."

"And while you were walking, did you walk to the bridge?"

"No, I did not," said my uncle, "for I tell you my way lay in the other direction. I walked through the town and back to our camp off the road to Evesham, and as soon as I reached our tents, I went to bed and soon to sleep. I did not see Edmund Speight again after leaving the Swan."

"Very well," said the coroner. My uncle turned away, but the coroner told him to wait a bit. Then the old man made a tent of his fingers and stared over it. "Now, the doctor's and Master Shakespeare's testimony raises a question that we must settle. Was the document that Edmund Speight had them witness truly a will? People in the tavern have said you might shed light upon that question."

My uncle shrugged. "How should I know that, Your Honor? It might have been a will. When we passed his farm, he and one of his sons were quarreling, and Speight did threaten to go into town and change his will."

"But we understand that the document was not discovered on Speight's body," the coroner said.

Giles Speight stood again. "It's plain to me. My father was going to take my brother, Francis, out of his will," he said. "I was to have everything."

Francis sprang up and, in a voice of outrage, said, "You cannot know that, no more than I can! And why should he leave you everything?" He turned to the townspeople in the room. "Everyone in town knows Father never forgave Giles for refusing to mow the high meadow last year! True, Father changed his will many times in the past, but you all know he drove my brother from the farm for the second time not more than a month ago!"

"And before he drove me out, he railed at you for courting Julia Cabot!"

"Yes, but even before that—"

"Quiet! Let us have order!" said the high-voiced coroner. "If there is no will, it is a simple matter. The estate and land must be settled upon the older son, as the law prescribes."

"Aye, that's just the rub," Constable Taylor burst out. "No one knows who was first-born, Giles or Francis. Only their father and mother were there the day the twins were born, and their mother died years ago. Sometimes old Edmund claimed Francis was born first by two minutes, and sometimes it was the other way, he said—Giles was two minutes older than his brother. It depended on how angry Edmund felt at one or the other of the boys at the time!"

"Then finding the proper heir might indeed prove to be a problem," the coroner said. He shrugged and added, "At any rate, that is a matter of law and of equity, and if there proves to be a will, it does not matter which is the older brother. Our business here is to judge what caused Edmund Speight's death." He then called Dr. Wells back again and asked him if he had taken note of when Edmund Speight had left the inn.

"I heard him quarrel with the player fellow," the doctor said carefully. "And then I think he drank a half-pint of sack."

"Only a half-pint?" asked the justice, sounding surprised.

Someone in the room said, "He wouldn't have paid for a drop more, sir," and everyone laughed save the Speight twins.

"He drank his wine," said the doctor. "That would have taken him a few minutes. He came to me and told me what he needed, and I had John Shakespeare join me to witness his signature, as you have heard. After that, I suppose he limped on out—he was lame in the left leg, you know—but I did not notice his going."

The justice then summed up the evidence for the jurors. He droned on and on, and at the end of his speech the jury conferred for hardly a minute before rendering their verdict: Edmund Speight, they said, had been foully murdered at the hands of a person or persons unknown. The coroner accepted their verdict and was on the point, it seemed, of adjourning the inquest when a sharp sound of voices drew everyone's attention to the door at the far end of the long room.

To my surprise, two stout young men dragged in thin, writhing old Ben Fadger, with him cursing and snapping and squirming every step of the way down the aisle and right up to the floor in front of the coroner's table. Ben stood glaring like a madman, mumbling and grumbling the way he always did.

"By your leave, Your Honor," one of the men said, "acting on the word of the sexton, we found this old man a-burning this in the players' camp outside of town." And he dropped onto the table the head and part of the shaft of a charred walking-stick. I knew it at once: It was the knotted, knobbly length of oak my uncle habitually carried.

And then the young man who had brought it in said, "Your Honor, the stick has blood on it."

Seven

"Bring in the evidence."

The coroner said for the second time, "Benjamin Fadger, do you understand the oath you have taken to tell only the truth?" He sounded stern and angry, as many people did when trying to make sense of Ben's grumblings and groaning.

Ben stared at him with red-hot fury. "Be ye deaf, ye old, long-beaked buzzard? Have I not already said yes, and curse you for leavin' them two young beasts to shake me so and haul my old bones this way and that, an' them not respectful of their elders, no, not one blasterd bit—"

"Make him be quiet, you watchmen! Answer me, then, if you understand the question," piped the coroner. "What is this piece of wood?"

Ben drew himself up to his full height, which was not as much as mine, and snorted loudly through his nose. "Marry, 'tis what the learned calls 'a stick.' I were burnin' it to cook my breakfast over, wasn't I? All broke up, it was not worth a farthing to nobody, but nice and dry, so I thought—"

"Where did you find it?" the coroner insisted, waving away Ben's words as if they were buzzing wasps.

"Why, 'twas on the path to the river, where I had to walk for water, wasn't it? There it was, broke as ye see and a-lying in the way, underfoot, ready to trip up poor old Ben Fadger, and his legs already as rheumatical stiff as two dry toasts. . . ."

The coroner again told the men to make Benjamin Fadger be quiet—they finally settled instead for dragging him to the door and outside—and then, holding the charred piece of wood up for all to see, the official asked the room at large, "Has anyone seen this stick before?"

An uneasy-looking Richard Hill raised his hand most reluctantly, I thought. "By your leave, sir, I believe that is the top part of a walking-stick carried by the chief of the players who came here yesterday."

The coroner called again on my uncle, who came forward, looked at the wood, swallowed hard, and said that, yes, it looked like the head of his stick.

"I never broke that stick, though," Uncle Matthew insisted. "'Twas whole the last time I saw it."

"And exactly when did you see it last?" the coroner asked.

My uncle frowned, sweat glistening on his big, broad, red face. Slowly he replied, "I had it when we built the stage you sit upon, sir, yesterday. I do not recall whether I took it from here at the end of our work."

But Dr. Wells rose at that and said, yes, he did remember seeing that same stick in my uncle's hands later in the tavern, just before Edmund Speight had come in looking for his lawyer or, failing him, for witnesses. Others agreed, and the long and the short of it was that in the end, Constable Taylor arrested both my uncle and old Ben under suspicion of murder and of destroying the evidence of murder.

I felt deathly sick at heart, and it was all I could do to keep from weeping or crying out. I lay on my stomach with my teeth clenched on the linen of my shirt sleeve—Ben Fadger would have clouted me on the head had he seen the way I abused his needlework—to keep my mouth shut and my voice still. Below me, the coroner said the inquest was over and that it was time for Stratford to return to its business.

And then as the men below us were all standing to leave, the Speight twins began to quarrel and rage, and they had to be held apart by four strong men as they shouted accusations and insults at each other. The constable and his helpers took them out separately, then busily cleared the room of chattering spectators, who were already rehearsing the tales they would tell in the taverns that evening.

As soon as everyone had left, Will swung like a long-legged monkey down through the open trapdoor, hung dangling to and fro by his hands for a moment, and then dropped to the stage beside the coroner's table, landing lightly on all fours like a cat and making hardly more noise than if he had been one. I followed, keeping my balance on two feet when I hit the stage. "What are we to do?" I wailed. "My uncle arrested! He would do no murder—I know him, Will! My uncle a murderer! Why, he has no temper at all, nor is he ever in ill humor! Matthew Bailey is a fellow of lively jest, of excellent fancy, of good will!"

"Shh, shh," hissed Will. "No more of that, no more, I pray you! Keep your voice down. I believe you, Tom—oh, see here, I cannot go on calling a girl 'Tom.' 'Tis—'tis impious and unnatural! Pray tell me, then, what is your real name? If you fear me for an informer, tell me only your Christen name, but tell me true."

What point was there in holding that back now? If Matthew Bailey was lost to me, I was as good as lost to all the world. "Viola," I admitted.

"A good name," Will said, though I suspected him of spouting flattery just to keep me quiet. "A sweet name, and it suits you well. Viola, then, we will save your uncle, I promise we will, and find the real murderer. My hand on it!"

We clasped hands, and for a very short moment I thought this mad village boy might be my only friend and my only hope in all the wide world. Then my mind cleared, I saw things as they really were and not as my sick heart painted them, and I said bitterly, "What, we two ungrown youths track down a murderer? If we did, who would believe us? And how should we even begin to set about such a task?"

"If we do find the murderer, we shall also find the evidence," Will insisted. "And we will be sure to seek such proofs as shall make it clear as a sunrise on a cloudless day that your uncle bears no blame for the death of Edmund Speight. How do we begin? Why, we start at the task, I think, by learning what we can about Francis and Giles Speight. Mark me, I think that whoever struck Edmund Speight on the head did so to steal that will he carried."

"We don't even know that there *was* such a will."

"What else could the papers that my father and Dr. Wells witnessed be but a will? Trust me, Tom—Viola, I mean—one of those two brothers must have seen it as a wicked will. If Francis thought he was to be cheated of his inheritance by his ill-tempered brother—or, more like to my mind, if evil-tempered Giles thought his father might with that will be giving land and money and all to Francis—one of the two of them would have cause to take and burn that piece of paper. It was the will that got Edmund killed, and that I know as surely as I know your name—*both* your names!"

"That makes sense," I conceded. "But what if the will did rouse the brothers' anger? It would be no cause for anyone to suspect Matthew Bailey! My uncle would have no reason to care who inherited old Speight's money and lands."

"Exactly!" Will's brown eyes glittered. "Why, look you: 'tis plain to me what happened. The killer wanted someone else to take the blame and the punishment for his evil deed so that no one would ever pry into what he was doing, and where, and when, and with whom. He would have someone to be judged in his place, a scapegoat. Now, who would better suit that role than a strolling player, new to Stratford, and even better, one that half the town had seen quarrel with Speight? That's why someone stole his stick and killed old Speight with it! All that remains—"

"Yes?"

He looked sheepish as he admitted the discouraging truth: "All that remains is for us to prove it so."

Eight

"And on this couple drop
a blessed crown!"

The forenoon had grown old with the inquest. As Will and I stepped out of the Guild Hall, I heard my name called, and there at hand was Peter Stonecypher. He led me aside and said, "Son, I know not whether you have heard the sad news. Your uncle's taken up and bound in prison, for suspicion of murder, and Ben Fadger's arrested with him. Alan's riding Molly down to London to tell Master Burbage and perhaps fetch back money for a lawyer. The rest of us are determined like iron to wait it out and help Matthew all we can—but what is to be done with you?"

Will had been dancing about not far away. "Oh sir, sir!" he exclaimed. "My mother and father will take Tom in. They are fond of children, and the two of us have become friends.

Let Tom stay with us, do—the Shakespeares, in Henley Street. Fine and delicate work in gloves and leather!" When Stonecypher looked dubious, Will went on: "Oh sir, do say yes. Another mouth to feed is nothing, for I have two brothers and two sisters, and what is a sixth when there are already five?"

Perhaps Will's mention of "another mouth to feed" decided him, for Peter was in charge of our purse, and I knew it was none too heavy. "If your parents give their consent, so be it," he said. To me, he added, "Tom, we will let you know when word comes back from Master Burbage, and if we must move on, we will either take you with us or be sure that you are well set up here. And you keep out of trouble and obey your elders, do you hear?"

"Yes, sir," I said.

As soon as he had left us, Will said, "Master Burbage? Why not to Lord Edgewell, since you are his players?"

"Lord Edgewell is not a rich man," I told him. "Yet he longs for the pomp of being a sponsor of a playing-troupe. We work oftentimes for Master James Burbage, who pays us well."

That seemed to satisfy Will, who hurried me along to his house, where his mother, a cheerful, comfortable-looking, stoutish woman, heard him out as he spun a sad tale: "Tom's mother and father are dead, and his uncle Matthew is lying in prison, innocent though Lord knows what is to happen to him, and he has nothing in the world, nor no one to watch out for him, and what is to become of him? Should he starve in the streets?"

Mary Shakespeare rolled her eyes and said, "Of course not! He can sleep and eat with us for the nonce, and now go and wash your hands, for dinner is this minute on the table."

The Shakespeare table was a crowded and rowdy one, with Mrs. Shakespeare at one end, the pink-faced John at the head, and the older Shakespeare children on either side— Will, the oldest, and then Gilbert, Joan, and five-year-old Anne, with the two-year-old Richard sitting on his mother's lap and sharing from her plate, or treen, rather, a countrified wooden platter, for I gathered they had no expensive pewter. I squeezed in beside Will, and the young servant brought us food and drink, a savory meat pie and small beer that, because it lacked the tang of alcohol, I supposed, made John Shakespeare frown and sigh.

To my surprise, as we finished, the master of the house called me aside and muttered, "Tom, lad, I'm right sorry for your uncle. To my mind he seems an honest man. When Lawyer Collins comes back from Oxford, I shall speak to him. We will see your uncle receives a fair English trial, I promise you."

I nodded my gratitude, unwilling to trust my voice, which threatened to quaver under the weight of this unexpected charity from a Catholic couple. "Father," Will said, "we have to fetch Tom's clothes. May we go now?"

"Aye," said John Shakespeare. "And keep out of mischief, do you hear? Never fear, Tom. Worst come to worst, you're welcome to share our bed and board, and we'll find some work for you to do here in the town."

On the way to our camp, Will asked, "Why do you look so sad, Viola?"

"You heard your father," I told him. "I'll share his house and meals, and he'll find work for me. He does not expect that my uncle will get off."

"Father never expects much that comes true," Will said cheerfully enough. "I tell you again, never fear! You and I will find the key that unlocks your uncle's prison door!"

"I want to see him."

"And you shall, but first things first."

It took very little time for me to bundle up my clothes and bid farewell to a moody-looking Watkyn Bishop and Michael Moresby. They tried to cheer me up—"Ah, never worry, Master Tom, soon enough Alan will be back from

London with money from Burbage, and then we'll hire your uncle a proper attorney."

I pretended to believe them, not wanting to add to their own woes by piling my worries atop theirs. As we walked back to the Shakespeares', Will asked, "Who is this James Burbage, the man you ask for help? A kind man who loves the theater?"

I laughed. "Kind? I know not whether many would call him that, but James Burbage is an actor and businessman in London, and yes, he does love the theater. He has his own troupe of actors, whom we often join with when their plays are large ones. Lord Edgewell is on excellent terms with Master Burbage, and though my Lord Edgewell has little riches of his own, he is friendly with a good many wealthy men and he helped Master Burbage gain the money for his great investment. He has just built a—"

The doleful toll of a funeral bell cut me short. Will's eyes flashed. "Edmund Speight is being buried!" he exclaimed. "Quick, let's drop off your bundle and run to the church!"

We popped in and out of the Shakespeare house before Mary Shakespeare could so much as speak to her son, and then we pelted in a most unmournerly manner down the street and off to the church. I saw we had small reason for such haste: The pallbearers were just taking the coffin inside.

At the far side of the churchyard, the mad sexton, Coste, stood more than waist-deep in an open grave.

"One foot deeper and he will begin to toss up bones," Will whispered to me. It was the custom to evict skeletons from old graves to make room for new bodies. The skeletons would be taken apart and stored in the charnel house, the stone building at the side of the church that seemed to frighten Will so much. Coste did not appear to notice us, and to be sure we gave him small chance to do so, edging around to the church door very quietly.

We stepped just inside. Will whispered that he was surprised to see so many mourners for old Speight, who was not well liked in Stratford, "but," he added, "we haven't had many murders."

Even so, the church was less than a quarter full. The minister read from the doleful English burial service: "We brought nothing into this world, neither may we carry anything out of this world. The Lord giveth, and the Lord taketh away. Even as it hath pleased the Lord, so cometh things to pass. Blessed be the name of the Lord."

When the service ended, the pallbearers brought the coffin our way, and Will dragged me out of the door and around the corner of the church. We saw Francis and Giles Speight following the coffin—though I could no more tell which was which than I could tell the difference between two fresh-minted pennies.

We crept around behind the church and from its shelter spied the pallbearers lowering the miserly old man to his eternal rest. Then one of the Speight sons walked briskly away toward town. The other lingered in company with a young woman clad in a black mourning dress. "Francis, for sure," Will whispered to me. "For that is Julia Cabot of Snitterfield. Here they come! Be quiet!"

We pressed against the stone wall of the church, and soon I heard a woman's voice, soft, sweet, and worried: "I care not if you possess money and land or nothing at all, Francis. If you will have me, I'll be your wife, and what little I bring with me is yours. We will make our way in the world somehow."

And then Francis's voice, which I recalled from our first meeting: "Julia, I want you to be happy as a queen, and as little in want as any good wife of the parish. Yes, I want to marry you, but pray have patience, my life and my darling. In a few days we shall know whether I am to have a share in my father's estate or not. Then we can make our wedding plans."

"I wish you would not hesitate so. What if the court grants you all of your father's money and lands? Then people will say that poor Julia Cabot, whose father can give her little, is marrying you for love of your fortune. Or what if they say you are to have nothing? Then they will cry out that Julia Cabot marries you from mere pity! Take me as your wife now, Francis, and let them say I marry your hazards as well as your hopes, that I am willing to take any chance, so I be by your side."

They were quiet for so long that Will peeped around the corner. He drew his head back with a squashed, sick expression, as if a beetle had flown into his mouth. "They're *kissing*," he whispered in disgust.

"I love you dearly," Francis's voice came at last. "But, Julia, we cannot marry so soon. For one thing, I am sure to be called as witness in that fellow's trial."

"The man who killed your father?"

"God forgive you," said Francis quickly. "I don't believe that player had the least thing in the world to do with Father's death, though I'll grant that Father had the kind of sharp tongue that would make many a man willing to shut him up by rapping him on the head. I spoke to Master Bailey, and he seemed to be a fellow of no hot humors, not the kind to be roused to anger that would lead to man-killing."

"But the stick was his."

"Aye, the stick was his, but who can say that the stick

ended my father's life? It might as well have been a stone or a branch of a tree, they say. Or if the stick was the weapon, who can say that the player was the one who held it? There are too many questions, Julia, too many mysteries to allow us to marry just at present. But I do love thee, perdition take my soul if I do not love thee, and here's my promise"—now I could hear the soft smacks of their kissing, for they had come very close—"and here's my bond, that as soon as ever may be, I shall take you to church and make you my wife."

Will grabbed my sleeve and dragged me away from the church wall and said loudly, "Don't worry, Tom, for if your uncle is innocent—oh, give you good day, Master Francis, and sorry we are for your heavy loss."

We had met them face-to-face. I looked at Julia Cabot and wished that when I acted young marriageable girls onstage I could look half as beautiful as she. She was blond, short, and just plump enough, with a fetching face and the most lovely blue eyes. Now she blushed becomingly as Will bowed to her and elbowed me to do the same. "Good day to you, Mistress Cabot," he said. "I hope your father thrives."

"Well, I thank you, Will," Julia Cabot said, smiling at the young fellow aping the manners of a gentleman.

"This is Tom Pryne," Will said to her, "nephew to that Matthew Bailey who has been arrested. Tom is sure his uncle is innocent, and I was telling him that our court will give him a fair trial."

"That it shall," said Francis, ruffling my hair. "Never worry, lad. I tell thee here, before God, I think thy uncle an innocent man, and what help I can be, that I shall be."

"Thank you, sir," I muttered, doubting whether even the murdered man's son could be much help in our trouble. "And I hope you may be blessed for your charity."

We parted company with them, and Will led me past the whipping-post and the stocks to the jail in High Street where my uncle and Ben Fadger had been locked up. None of the four town constables was about, but a young fellow of the watch who was a deputy led us back and let us into the strong cell that held the two prisoners.

My uncle sprang up from his cot the instant he saw me, his face showing relief but not happiness. "Tom!" he exclaimed, sweeping me into his arms for an embrace while the deputy locked us all in. "God be thanked. I wondered what had become of you!"

"I told you he would be all right," grumbled Ben, scratching himself as he sat on his own bed, a wooden platform covered with a villainous-looking sack of straw as mattress. "Young 'uns have nine lives, like unto a cat, and they always lands also on their feets, so they does."

Will hastily told Uncle Matthew of our arrangements, and my uncle gravely thanked him. "Now," Will said, "to business, and that quickly, before Constable Taylor comes back and throws us out, for that's what he probably will do. Tell us about that stick—how came it to be broken, and why did Master Fadger burn it, and tell us true. It may mean your lives, so quickly tell us everything!"

My uncle looked from Will to me in silent, round-eyed astonishment. I shrugged. "I think you'd better do as he asks, Uncle," I said. "For like it or hate it, I think Will is the best chance you have of escaping the hangman."

❧ Nine ❧

". . . 'tis like the breath of an unfee'd lawyer . . ."

"I do not know," my uncle confessed in response to Will's hurried questioning. "Before Heaven, I do not know whether I left my stick in the tavern or not. I had drunk a good deal, Master Will, and my head reeled with beer. Then too, I knew I had to hurry to camp, for by remaining in town as late as I had, I courted being arrested."

Will grunted and shook his head. "Nay, I think not, sir, for Constable Taylor is not a man to stick to the letter of the law, not when things are going smoothly. I think you could sit and drink quietly far into the night, and never would he bother you—but the stick, sir, that is important! Try to remember all you can about where you lost it, and how!"

Uncle Matthew frowned, his red face creasing into lines

of thought. "I do recall that once out of the Swan and into the cool air, I sorely needed to leak. I have some memory of propping my stick against the tavern wall near the door as I slunk into the shadows, but whether or not I picked it up again after that, I honestly do not recall. I recall nothing distinctly after that until I reached camp and all but fell into my bed, and that is the truth."

Will nodded, then turned to Ben Fadger. "And where and how did you find this stick, and in what condition?"

Ben looked at him with an intensely vacant expression. "Hold, lad, I don't know what you means, with your wheres and your hows and your conditions."

I could tell that it was an effort for Will not to raise his voice: "One at a time, then. Where did you find the stick you burned?"

"Oh, that. 'Tis as I told that fat-brained bald-pated sharp-nosed vulture-eyed pile of old—"

"Yes, I know you told the crowner you found it whilst going down to the river for water," broke in Will, all impatience.

"Aye, and so I did: three dozen yards o' walking, and me with a heavy pail to haul, and there it lay, that wicked piece of wood, on the path down to the water, and I knew it at once for half o' Master Matthew's stick—"

"Half?" Will asked. "Half? Do you mean it really was broken already?"

"Which I said it was—maybe two foot of it left, and that in the path to the river, where it would roll out from under poor old Ben's feet, or catch between his legs to trip a body up—"

I almost had to laugh because as it seemed to me, for the first time in his life young Will Shakespeare had run into someone who could pour out even more words than he could. "Please," Will said urgently, "tell us just where you found it!"

Ben scratched his nose, as if his brain lay in it and he were trying to stir it up to think. "Marry, it were but a few steps from the water. I could see the church off to my left, maybe a hundred or two hundred steps away, no more than that. Anyhow, I picked the old broke stick up, so did I, thinking, Master Matthew will be that angry at someone a-breakin' of his stick, but seein' as we needed wood for the fire and it was good stout oak, I thought, thought I, 'twill serve for fuel, any road, and so I brought it back to camp. And not long after them two bully-monsters, them puffed-up hulks with more brawn than brain, them—"

What more they were we were not to learn, for at that point the outer door flew open and Constable Taylor's loud, grating voice ordered, "Out of there, Will! Out of there, you two young pestilences!"

Five minutes later, with our ears burning from the constable's shouted rebukes, Will and I found ourselves on the street again. "Come," he said, seeming not a bit discouraged. "Follow me."

And he led me to a good brick house, a bigger one than the run of homes in Stratford. He went round to the back, led me through a gate that opened into a green growing garden, and pounded on the back door of the house. When a young serving girl opened it, he said, "Delia, is Lawyer Collins back yet?"

"Don't call me 'Delia'!" She was black-haired and black-eyed and about my age, some two years older than Will, but unlike me, she had already the figure and the fine confident flashing anger of a woman grown. "He is back from Oxford, Will Shakespeare, but he has no errands for you to run, so good day to you!"

"Wait, wait!" Will put his foot in the closing door and wedged it open. "Delia—Cordelia—let us in, do. This is Thomas Pryne, actor, come all the way from London town, and 'twould be a shame not to let such a far-traveled boy in to meet your master."

"Actor?" Cordelia said, opening the door and gazing

at me. "One of those with the man they have taken for murdering old Mr. Speight?"

"He is my uncle," I told her.

"Poor lad!" She sighed. "To think I might have been one of the last to see Edmund Speight alive! He came riding up on that great ambling bay gelding of his and pounded on the door, calling for my master. How angry he was when I told him Mr. Collins had gone to Oxford! He shook his fists and limped away, and I had to help him back into the saddle, though he swore at me, and he rode off in foul temper. He must have been killed not long after!"

" 'Tis most important that we see your master now," Will importuned.

"I tell you, my master is busy!" Cordelia insisted, but her black eyes flicked toward me with something of an expression of interest. She pouted, and I wished that onstage I could show such cherry-red lips as she had. "What business do the likes of you have with him, anyway? Does it have to do with Mr. Speight?"

"We just want to speak with Master Collins for a minute, Cordelia, that's all."

She stood hesitating, blocking the open doorway so we could not pass inside. Then, shyly, she said, "Do you really act in plays, young master?"

"I really do," I said. "I play the women's parts, for I am young in my craft, and that is how we are apprenticed."

She smiled. "You'd make a pretty young woman, I warrant. You have a pleasing face, Master Tom."

I bowed to her. "Such praise from such a beauty is praise indeed," I replied, trying to fill my voice with honey, the way Alan did when he acted the part of a young lover.

With a charming pink blush she murmured, "Well ... I will let you in, but you must wait until my master has finished with his business. He is sitting this minute with the crowner, and they are not to be disturbed."

"We shall be quiet as two dumb mice," promised Will, and the girl showed us in. We entered through a larder, well stocked and fragrant with the aromas of hanging hams, dried apples, and other delicacies. I thought that whatever else Lawyer Collins might be, he was a man who treated his stomach kindly.

"You'll wait here," Cordelia said firmly, showing us into a kind of cramped little butler's cubby. "I have to finish cleaning upstairs. I'll be back in a few minutes, and you mind you be quiet as you promised, you rogue of a Will."

Will mimed locking his lips and pocketing the key, and with a giggle and another friendly glance at me, head to toe, Cordelia left us. Will leaned close and whispered, "She fancies you, *Tom*!"

"Oh, go to!" I snapped, not half amused.

"When she comes back, ask her for one kiss, just one kiss. If she does not grant it, then I'm a—ouch! Don't pinch me like that!"

"Then don't vex me!"

"Not so loud! To our business, then. Come, for we are in better luck than I'd hoped. Quiet, now—follow me and walk a-tiptoe!"

I noticed how cat-quiet Will could be when he wanted. He led me down a dark hallway lined with shelves full of dusty old books that I smelled more than saw, that spicy scent of old leather tickling my nose. At the far end of the hall, doors led to the left and right, and the one on the right was open just a crack, letting a little wedge of light stream across the rush-strewn floor and run up to touch the spines of more books on the shelves at our left shoulders.

As we edged up to the door I could hear the high-pitched, reedy voice of the coroner: ". . . the man may indeed have made out a new will, sir. That is what the people of this town want to know, and I am bound to say that if he did, and if we knew the content of that new will, my views on the fellows we have in jail might possibly change. We all wish to see justice done, I hope." He sniffed, which made me want to sniff in sympathy, but I feared that I would sneeze, so infernally book-dusty was the passage in which Will and I stood.

Another man, presumably Lawyer Collins, then spoke in a deeper voice and in a deliberate, slow way, his tongue loving the terms of his profession: "I understand you, sir, I understand you. However, it is a *sine qua non* of law and equity that a man and his solicitor must place perfect trust and faith in each other, and keep a solemn understood agreement not to divulge what passes between them in the way of consultation. I can tell you, however, that Master Speight did indeed have a will, made by me, and in the absence of any later will, that one shall be probated, and then *res ipsa loquitur*—the thing speaks for itself, I mean."

The coroner sounded positively peevish at that: "Aye, but what if the witnesses were right? What if Speight had made out another will, or a codicil to the old one? Would that, if found, supersede the one you made for him?"

The lawyer chuckled. "The *ones* I made for him, sir, for to tell the truth, Edmund Speight changed his will more often than some men change their breeches! Why, in this past year alone I have writ out no fewer than five wills, the first favoring one son, the second the other, the third the first—that one lasted not even a week!—and then for a short time both sons with rough equality, and then the second son alone! Now you tell me of a new will, a sixth one! Should a holograph will, and by that I mean one in the man's own handwriting, for he could read and write, sir, should such a handwritten document exist and be duly witnessed, aye, it would very likely stand in court as representing the *decedent's* wishes concerning his heirs and property."

"And it might show who would want Master Speight dead," said the coroner.

The lawyer agreed: "Yes, knowing the content of that holograph or self-written will, if it exists, would tell us *cui bono,* who benefits, yes, I understand you. However, I know nothing of that."

"That is the reason," said the coroner, "why I ask you about the previous will, the one in your keeping. For if he changed it, then by seeing the old will we might be able to hazard a guess about what the new one contained!"

In his deeper voice, the lawyer rumbled, "I am sorry that, in accordance with the dictates of my profession, sir, I cannot show you the will I wrote for Speight not quite a month ago. Still, I see your dilemma. Without divulging details, sir, I may just hint that, should the will that I hold in my office stand, why, then, one of Speight's sons will do quite well, and the other be disappointed. The one who benefits under that will, sir, is—"

I sneezed.

Will grabbed my arm and made no pause but hurled me down the passage, through the butler's cubby, and out the back door. "Run!" he said. We raced to the tall wooden fence around Lawyer Collins's back garden, flashed over it, and crouched like young rabbits in the tall grass on the far side, hidden from view.

Behind us we heard Collins's angry voice thundering from the back door: "Who is there? Who is there? Be warned, villains! I'll bring the law on you! What, you break into the house of a man of law? Will you make a younker of me, rogues? Be warned!" The door slammed, and Will let out a long breath.

He gave me a long, irritated look. "Viola, your nose may be perfect for acting the part of a marriageable young girl, but curse it for a secret-breaker! One more moment and we should have known how Speight planned to change his will!"

"I'm sorry!" I said.

"No matter," he mumbled. "There must be another way. There must be. And trust me to think of it!"

I did not trust him much at all, but having thrown in with him, I felt obliged to see it out. "I know you will," I said, using all my acting skills to speak a lie and make it sound like truth.

ᴥ **Ten** ᴥ

"... there is a devil haunts thee ..."

No matter what young Will's intentions were, for the rest of that Friday he thought of no trick, no shift that would tell us of the will. And that afternoon his mother caught us as we passed the house and set us to work cleaning the leather shop, which Will's father would not allow a servant to touch. We dusted the shelves and arranged the goods John Shakespeare had in stock—some dainty ladies' gloves in white kidskin, cut out but unstitched so they could be sized when bought, and some sturdy men's calfskin riding gloves, and a few odds and ends of other work, including some ingenious pouches and wallets.

At present more than a dozen sacks of wool stuffed most of the office, for in addition to his work as a craftsman of leather, John Shakespeare bought and sold wool and grain. When we had finished and were called in to the evening meal, Will's father told of the attempt of house-breakers to rob Lawyer Collins that day. By that time the tale had grown monstrously, so that the poor two of us youngsters had been changed in the telling to a band of half-a-dozen broad-shouldered robbers armed with swords and pistols, whom Mr. Collins had held off in desperate fight.

"I believe not a word of it," declared Mary Shakespeare. "A half-dozen men on fat Mr. Collins! These lies are as gross as the man who tells them."

John Shakespeare shrugged. " 'Twas what he said. Perhaps we should look well to the doors tonight, to make sure they are secure."

"Father," said Will, "what about all the wool you have in the shop?"

His father's face clouded. "Aye, that could tempt a thief sure enough, for wool is fetching a good price right now."

"Here's a thought," said Will. "Let me and Tom sleep there this night. That way, should we hear the tread of a robber, we could rouse the house and save your wool."

I had not the least notion of what Will meant by all that, until it was time to sleep, and then he explained: "We will have time for private talk this way. Else we'd have to sleep in the room with Gilbert, and he's forever listening and spying."

"Your father has a large family to provide for," I said.

"It would have been larger, but my two older sisters both died young," he said carelessly. "Now I am eldest, and if I had my way, I'd have a dozen more sisters and brothers, for the more there are of them, the less time my parents have to watch and scold me! But what of your family, Viola? How many brothers and sisters do you have?"

"None," I said. "I did have an older brother, my mother told me, but he died before he was a month old, so I never knew him."

"An only child!" Will said in a tone of wonder. "By my faith, you must feel lonely at times." He was quiet for a minute, a sure sign he was thinking of something, and then he burst out, "I'll be your brother! From this night forward, whoever is against you is against Will Shakespeare! You're my little sister and my friend, and I will stand by you in everything."

I laughed, but my heart felt touched. I wondered too, why Will persisted in regarding me as smaller than he—I was tall enough to see the top of his head when we stood side by side! Yet I made no objection, for his sympathy moved me. Except for my uncle, no one had said such kind-sounding words to me in nearly a year. In the dark we settled down on the woolsacks, he against the right wall, I against the left. Thinking forlornly of my uncle, still in his cell, I tried to fall asleep. Honestly I do not know whether I did or not, for sometime during that dark night a harsh voice roused me from my place. I went to the front window and peered out at the moonlit street, all deserted. A raggedy figure capered and danced down it, his voice sounding so insane that it made me shiver:

"Oh, he that hath but little wit,
With a hey! Ho! The wind and the rain,
Must make content with his fortunes fit,
For the rain, it raineth every day!"

"Costard," groaned Will, coming up behind me to peer out. "He's drunk again. He has no money, but he haunts about the Bear—that's the tavern that stands across the street from the Swan—and cracks dirty jokes and sings filthy tunes until the owner, Master Barber, or some of those fooled by the fool buy him drink. Where's he gone?"

I looked back out the window, but the sexton's cracked voice had fallen silent, and the moonlight lay silver on the cobbles, as empty as if he had dissolved away to nothing, like the Ghost in *Murder Aveng'd*. Will pressed his face against the glass next to mine—

"Yaarghh!" Coste had crept up to the shop, on all fours, I supposed, and suddenly reared up not a foot from our noses, his eyes rolling and foam dripping from his mouth. Will shrieked and fell back, and I scrambled away myself, alarmed at this madman's scream.

But Coste laughed his head off, staggering and reeling around and clutching his sides. He shook his finger at the window, though Will and I had scuttled so far back that I am sure he could not see us, and he shouted, "I'll have you, body and bones, Will Shakespeare! I'll lock you in a box! The worms shall taste your living flesh, and you'll beg and beg for death—"

Lantern light fell into the street, and from an upstairs window John Shakespeare yelled down, "Away with you, fool, before the constable takes you up!"

"I'd not send for the constable, had I fathered as you fathered!" Coste shouted back. "Thieves! Thieves! Thieves loose in Stratford!"

"Get away, I tell you," bellowed Will's father. "Talk to me of thieves! This is Stratford, man, not some lonely unprotected farmhouse! Go, Costard, for if I must come and see you off, I'll do it with a blow and a kick!"

Coste made an uncouth gesture, but he reeled away into an alley just down the street and vanished into the darkness. "Will," I said, "what did he mean?"

"Nothing," Will said, though he sounded worried. "He is just stirring up trouble, the way he always does."

"Do you think he might have seen us running from the lawyer's house this afternoon?"

"What would Costard be doing in that part of town? I think he was just being a devil and causing trouble. Let's go to sleep. It must be nigh midnight."

I have slept well and slept rough, have lain on a feather-bed of my own and on a pallet of dry grass beneath a drumming tent in a rainstorm. My dreams have been dreamed beneath cozy blankets and beneath ragged canvas. I am bound to say, though, that never have I had a softer bed or a better sleep than that I finally fell into that night, on a yielding bag of fresh-washed wool. If ever I have a fortune, I know what I want to stuff my mattresses! The night seemed short until we woke again. We broke our fast with a meal of porridge and some chewy apple-johns, dried apples left over from the winter, and before either John or Mary Shakespeare could find any task for us to do, Will led me outside again.

"There's one who can find out the name that's in the old will," he said. "In fact, there are two, and both are named

Speight. If we can persuade them both to ask Lawyer Collins, we'll know as well as they who gets the lands and the money and who gets left out."

Finding Giles Speight, the harsh-tempered brother, proved easy, for since his father had cast him out of the house he had taken lodgings with Mr. Waterman, the owner of the Swan, and worked for him and some other people in town keeping books of account, for he had some education and wrote a fair hand and could add and subtract with the best of them.

We saw him as he came out of the Swan with his ledger-book under his arm, and Will gave him a jaunty greeting: "Give you good morning, Master Giles."

Giles Speight glanced at him and merely grunted in return. Will danced along at his side. "Carry your ledger for you?"

"It's no burden," Giles snapped. "Off with you boys now."

"We hear your brother will be rich soon," Will said. "We hear that since no one can find your father's new will, the old one still holds, and that it gives Francis all the money, and you shall have nothing but a little piece of land."

Giles Speight stopped dead in his tracks, glaring, his reddish hair gleaming in the sun, his face flushed with anger.

"What's that! Who told you? The will is to be read Monday. How did you—"

"Rumor wags a thousand tongues, they say," Will told him. "Good day, Master Giles."

Then we took a long tramp out into the countryside, to the farmhouse where now Francis Speight lived alone. He answered our knock and raised his eyebrows in surprise. "Why, Will Shakespeare! And the young player, I think—"

"Tom, sir," I said, bowing.

"Tom, yes. Why have you come all this way on a warm June morning?"

Will looked serious. "Francis, you've been like a big brother to me. You've taught me how to fish, and how to hunt, and a thousand other things. So when we heard, Tom and I, I said, 'We have to go and tell Master Francis.'"

"Tell me what?" the young man asked with a quizzical smile. He was handsome when he smiled like that, handsome in a way his sour-faced brother could never be, and once more I understood why a pretty girl like Julia Cabot could find love in her heart for such a sturdy young fellow.

Will dropped his voice to a conspirator's whisper: "They do say that Lawyer Collins has told your brother that the old will, the one your father made with him not long since, will hold as long as the new one is not to be found. And the whisper is that the old will gives you some money, but your brother all the land!"

"What?" Francis looked thunderstruck. "But Giles is no farmer, nor wants to be! By the Lord, I could do without the money if I had the farm, but t'other way around is plain madness!"

"Aye," said Will. "I know not whether it be true, but if you are to be moved out of your house and home, 'twould be well to be prepared."

"Wait a bit," Francis said, his face dark with anger. "I'll hitch up the gelding and you can ride into town in the wagon with me. They've no right to be gossiping about my family and my business. I'll soon put this right."

We followed him to the barn, where two horses waited in stalls, one a huge bay-colored gelding, the other a much smaller and older gray mare. Francis hitched the gelding to a little wagon, and we rode four miles to the bridge and to Stratford. As we rumbled over the arched bridge, toward the bar gates (which still stood open), something heavy hit the wagon behind us, and I jerked my head around. "Master Speight!" I said in alarm. "The sexton's boarded the wagon!"

The gray-haired Coste had leaped from nowhere, it seemed, and now clung to the back of the wagon, leering.

"Young Speight's come to town with a couple of naughty lads!" he said. And then like a crow thinking it was a nightingale, he began to sing, a grating, hoarse, harsh song probably of his own invention:

> "What care you for a father's curse,
> So long as he puts money in thy purse?
> A young man goes from bad to worse,
> All because of the money in his purse!"

"Get off, Costard!" exclaimed Francis Speight angrily. "Get off before I stop and throw you off!"

With that, Coste let go and dropped back to the road, where he stood making a mocking bow. "As you will, Master Speight," he grated. "As you will! Pray be charitable to one who wishes to do you a good turn!"

"That fellow pops up everywhere you do not expect him," muttered Francis.

"Like the devil at prayers," agreed Will.

 Eleven

"A will! A wicked will . . ."

This time we came to the front door, not the back, of
Lawyer Collins's fine brick home, and not the pretty,
flashing-eyed Cordelia but a different serving girl let us in.
We stepped around a corner and into the same dark, dusty,
book-lined hallway we had already visited, and from the
open door of the room on our left came the angry sound of
Giles Speight's voice: "I have to know, sir! Law or no law, you
must give me some inkling!"

"And me," said Francis, stepping through the doorway.
I could see past him and for the first time got a glimpse of
Lawyer Collins. He was an immense fat man with a broad
pale face beneath which not one but two chins dangled
and quivered. His small blue eyes gleamed, looking like

two sapphires pressed down in dough by a mad baker's thumbs.

"So you both have come," he rumbled. "And both of you on the same errand and demanding the same information, no doubt: *cui bono?* That is to say, who benefits from your father's will?" Collins shook his big head, and his jowls quivered with the movement. "Young men, you are too hot of head and too light of heed! I tell you, this is not something done *a bene placito*, simply at your pleasure, but rather a *questio*, an inquiry, for the courts!"

"Aye, and when will the matter be settled?" asked Giles in a waspish impatient tone. "The old man is dead and is feeding the worms! What cares he for questions of law now? Why may you not prove the will today?"

"Because this will and testament," said the lawyer, brandishing a folded and sealed piece of parchment, "may not be his *last* will and testament! I tell you, until the matter of your father's murder has been settled in the courts, until it is sure that whatever he had two men witness is or is not a later will, and until we know whether that document does or does not still exist, then no one can say if this declaration holds force or no! And if it is null, then it is also void, and with no authority. Until that is settled as a matter of law and equity, young masters—"

All the while he had been speaking, the fleshy lawyer waved the folded parchment about. With a sudden snatch, Giles Speight leaped forward, seized it, broke the seal, and stepped back as the red-faced Collins tried to push his vast bulk up from the chair.

Giles snorted and tossed the parchment down on the desk. "I have seen enough," he said with a sneer. He turned to his brother and, in a voice dripping with venom, he said, "Francis, I regret to tell you that in this paper, Father left the farm and most of the money to me. You shall have only forty pounds, the two boggy acres, and the horses. When this comes to court, I promise that I shall be a good brother and help you pack up what things you wish to take out of my house." He pushed past Francis, then past us, without so much as a second glance, and stalked out the front door, slamming it rudely behind him.

Collins had retrieved the will, which he hastily thrust into a box. He then turned a small brass key, locking the box, and began to mop his flowing face with a handkerchief. "This is—I could be—you will not tell anyone?" he asked anxiously. "I should have stopped your brother, but he was so confoundedly quick—you will not tell anyone that I broke the trust of a client?"

Quietly, Francis said, "Sir, I will not, if in return you will answer me a question: Is what my brother said true? Does the parchment you locked in that box indeed cut me off with barely a shilling in my pocket and some useless land?"

Collins nodded, looking wretched and defeated. "Aye. 'Twas written not a month ago, when you first mentioned marrying the Cabot girl, when Edmund was in a towering rage against you. And—I can tell you this, for it is not in force any longer—the will before that one divided both money and land equally between the two of you, and the one before that disinherited Giles in favor of you. I've made many a will for Edmund Speight these past four years, and in only one did he treat both of his sons with something like fairness."

"I thank you, sir," said Francis softly, and we followed him out into the sunlight.

"If the new will turns up," Will said hopefully, " 'tis sure to name you heir, Francis! Why else would he have changed it?"

Francis Speight climbed up to the wagon seat. "Why, indeed?" he asked with a wan smile. "Though I cannot see how that would be possible, as angry as he has been with me these weeks past. He rated me the other day about Julia— why, Will, you were there with the players, you must have heard how he ranted and roared. I see no reason why he would have felt a sudden kindness toward me as he came into town to have a new will witnessed!"

We watched him roll away in his wagon, back to Bridge Street and the turning he would take to return to the Speight farm. Will and I followed slowly. One or two boys, freed from their tasks this Saturday noon, called out to him and invited him to come join them in sport or play, but Will waved them all off.

"What do—" I began, but Will waved me to silence.

"Don't talk for a while, but let me walk and think," he told me as we came back to the market square, bustling now with people. Some housewives were fetching water from the pump, others haggling with farmers who had brought hens, plump clucking capons, eggs, or other things for sale. Smaller children darted in and out of the crowd, playing hide-and-seek among the legs of their elders. Will twitched me by the sleeve, and I followed him around the edge of the throng, and then down past the Guild Hall and a chapel nearby, all the way down to the river.

On this sunny day I noticed, as I had not before, how pretty the Avon's banks were, sparkling with wildflowers of all hues: pied daisies, beautiful blue violets, ladies'-smocks, a dozen other kinds, orange and red, pink, and yellow. They all waved and danced in the light warm breezes, until you would have thought it a holiday for wildflowers. Only the smell was terrible. "What is that?" I asked, wrinkling my nose against the horrible, sulfuric stench. "An open sewer?"

"Hm? Oh, the Mere," Will said, his voice distant. "It's a filthy little stream that runs down across the bog there and into the river. It does have a nasty reek, like a rotten fen. It stinks like that wicked will."

"That's an unsavory simile," I muttered.

"I don't care. The will *is* rotten. Of course old Speight was supposed to have left his land to whichever of his sons is older, that's the law, but to cut the other one off with forty pounds and some bad pasture, why, that's devilish and evil and it stinks, Viola. Still, it is useful to know what was in Speight's old will, for you see what it means."

"It means that Francis is without luck," I said. "And it means that he and Julia probably cannot marry, not on just forty pounds. It means that the sour-faced old Speight has handed his home and his fortune over to the sour-faced young Speight."

"Not only that," said Will, all impatience. "It means that we now know beyond any doubt who the murderer is!"

"We do?" I stared at him, but he did not seem to be joking. "I know what you think—that the old will favored

Giles, and so Giles must be guilty. But that would hold true only if Giles *knew* about the wills, and he did not."

Will rounded on me with an expression of amazement. "It must be Giles," Will exclaimed, waving his arms, sawing the air in his excitement. "Why, look you, his father tossed him out of the house once before, last autumn because after mowing one meadow and being still all a-sweat and sore with the work, he would not mow a second when old Edmund ordered him to do it! Edmund took Giles back, but then last month they argued and Edmund threw him out again, expecting him to come creeping back to apologize. Giles is too proud, though. Since then he has been living hand to mouth, scraping out a living in town. Now, the murderer must have taken the new will—but it could not have named Giles heir, because the old one did!"

"But Francis and his father fell out! We saw them, we heard them! Old Edmund wouldn't have changed his will in favor of Francis."

"But he must have, because that is the only way he could have changed it! Don't you see? Old Edmund juggled his sons, one high, one low, and no doubt he wanted to hold out to Francis the lure of his lands and money—provided Francis would stop courting Julia Cabot!"

I didn't know whether Will had lost his mind or whether

I had lost mine. "That might be possible," I admitted. "But I tell you, Giles didn't *know* what was in the old will, not until he read it today. It might not have left him anything."

"You're right. Giles would have read the new will before he killed his father, and as for the old . . . I have it! Giles must have peeked at the will that Lawyer Collins has now! He must have known all about that one as well!"

"Then why did he seize the will from the lawyer just now?"

Will gave me the kind of pitying look one bestows on an idiot child. "Why, because he wanted his *brother* to know he had won, of course! And Giles wanted to hide the fact that he himself *already* knew what was in the will. Come, come, Viola, think! It must be that Giles had read that will. Don't you see? If Giles knew that he was his father's heir, and then heard that his father had come into Stratford to change his will—"

"Then he would know that Edmund must be changing the will to cut his share down or to cut him out," I said. "And he would have a reason to kill the old man and destroy the papers he carried."

"And they do say that Edmund Speight was asking all over town for Lawyer Collins, and that he was telling everyone he had a will to be witnessed," Will replied. "Word of what the old man was doing must have reached Giles. 'Tis not so hard to see what could have happened."

"And if Giles saw his father coming out of the Swan," I said slowly, "he might have seen my uncle come out too, and lean his stick against the wall—"

"Giles seizes the stick!" said Will, miming the action. "He runs after his father! He catches him alone on the far side of the bridge and, whack! Thwack!" He viciously swung his imaginary weapon with such ferocity that I flinched, thinking Will might be not so bad an actor himself, should he be inclined to try his luck upon the stage.

"What's this? The old man's dying fingers open, and something white flutters down to the ground!" Will picked up an imaginary document and thrust it inside his shirt. Then he said, "He seizes his father's body, lugs it to the bridge, and throws it over the parapet! Splash! Then he thinks of the stick—he broke it over his old father's head! He picks the pieces up. Which way? Not back toward his father's house, for he's not lived there in months. Not to his lodgings, not with the weapon in his hand. He hurries through the darkening streets, sneaking from shadow to shadow, out the south end of town, to the other bridge. He'll throw the broken stick into the water of the weir!" Will swung his arm back and mimicked an underhand toss. "He doesn't notice that half of the stick falls short! Then, thinking the evidence gone, he hurries back to his lodging, slips in, and burns the new will! The thing is done! But the deadly end of the stick lies in darkness on the path, where your old actor friend found it the next morning."

"I can see that happening," I agreed reluctantly, for in truth, Will's hot-headed imagination was as catching as a contagious fever. "But what good does it do us? If all you say is true, we have no way of proving it."

"Aye," Will said gloomily. "That's the rub, all right. We need more help than I can give you, Viola. We need . . ." He thought for a minute, and then his brown eyes lighted up. He smacked his right fist into his left palm. "Why, of course. We need—a ghost!"

◇ Twelve ◇

"Name what part I am for,
and proceed."

Peter Stonecypher, looking worried, sat outside one of the tents, talking to Watkyn Bishop. Beyond them, Dunce contentedly ate grass. "Tom," said Peter as I came near, "how is the life in the town, lad?"

"Well, I thank you," I said. "I suppose Alan is not yet back?"

"Nay," Watkyn said. "He may have got to London by this time, if Molly did not stagger and fall from his driving her so hard."

"Alan is a better rider than that," Peter said quickly. I knew that Molly would make but a slow journey of it, for she was not the youngest of animals. If we'd been in funds, Alan might have rented stronger post-horses along the way. 'Twas said that renting one horse after another, you could ride a hundred miles or more in a day. On slow Molly, though, Alan would be lucky to go more than twenty or so miles before she needed a long rest.

"How do you fare here in camp?" I asked.

With a sigh, Peter jingled the little leather purse that my uncle usually carried. It rang thinly. "We have not much brass, and that's the truth," he said. "Michael won us eighteen pence at shove-groat in the Bear, but now no one will play with him. We must make what we have last."

I could not keep from smiling. Shove-groat was a kind of shuffleboard, played on a table. A rectangle divided into nine parts, numbered from nine down to one, would be drawn in chalk. Then the players would toss for turn. Each one would put a coin—a King Edward shilling, old and worn smooth, for preference—at the edge of the table, so its rim just overhung. Then, with a quick slap, the player would send the coin sliding down onto the board.

You had to score nine on the first try. Then the goal was to send the coin onto numbers that would add up to thirty-one, no more and no less. You shot until you went over that number, or missed the board, or until your coin touched a line, and then you gave over your turn and waited, having to begin at nine all over again. Although most places had laws against wagering, people did bet with each other and with the players. Michael Moresby was an old hand at the game, and I could see how in one evening he could begin with but one penny and his favorite shooter, one of those old Edward shillings, and end with eighteen pence clinking in his pocket. Still, as Peter said, once the locals had lost bets to him, it would be hard for him to find another profitable game.

"I might be able to find some food for you," I said.

Peter smiled and ruffled my hair. "We can eat, lad. 'Tis idleness that is our curse. We practice lines from the plays, and we do the dances and the tumbling and all, but not working—that is a curse, when a man's willing to work." He sniffed. "This is Saturday. Alan would not set out on Sunday to return, and 'tis eighty mile or more, a weary journey. I look not to see him until Thursday next. I'll warrant we can hold out that long. May you stay with the family where you are lodged until then?"

"Aye," I said. "Master John Shakespeare is no child-despiser, and his wife is a kind woman. Still, if Alan returns with money, and if my uncle is released, I'd want to leave them a gift of money for their kindness."

"That's well said," Peter told me, though Watkyn, our comedian, looked woeful.

Watkyn said, "A stranger has been asking about your uncle, Tom."

Peter shushed him, but not before I felt a quiver of alarm. "A stranger?"

Peter said, " 'Tis neither here nor there—"

"Nay," I said, "tell me, pray. What did he want?"

With a shrug, Peter said, "I know not, lad, for he wouldn't speak to us. He was a youngish man, dark-haired and dark of face, like a foreigner, though the tongue in his head spoke English fair enough. He sought us out and said he had a message for Matthew, but on learning he was in jail, he left us without a word. Never mind. 'Tis probably someone wanting to ask about joining the company, for he had a kind of public air about him."

"His name?"

"He never told us."

With that new worry on my shoulders, I made an excuse about taking something to my uncle and went into our tent. A trunk there held the paints and wigs that we used. I pulled an empty sack from my shirt and made a quick selection, remembering how Michael, that beanpole of a man, used whites and greens and grays and blacks to make himself look like a skeleton, or like a ghost. A wig I took too, one cunningly made with a flesh-colored cap and a fall of gray around the ears. It would be large on me, but in darkness—which Will's scheme called for—it would pass.

I crept back out of the tent. Watkyn and Peter had put a cauldron on the campfire (the same cauldron, I noticed, that we used in *The Witches and the Warrior*) and were heating water, while Watkyn skinned a hare. I knew then that they were being very careful with the pennies—we ate wild food only when we had no brass with which to buy our bread and meat.

I bade them good evening and, my bag in hand, set off on the short walk toward Stratford town limits. I struck a path that led down to the river and, idly wondering about the place where Ben Fadger found the head of my uncle's stick, I turned off and followed it through green grass and a spray of yellow flowers. It curved just before reaching the riverbank. I could see that it came out just on the upstream side of the mill. Off to my right a barrier placed across the river made a weir, a low dam that created a smooth millpond. Beyond the weir, a narrow wooden footbridge crossed the river. Indeed, I had crossed it with Will on our first day in town. On the far side of the Avon, a half-dozen boys my age and upward to perhaps twenty fished from the bank. They gazed at me and spoke to one another. Not wanting to answer questions, I turned and walked back.

Francis Speight, Will had said, had taught him how to fish and swim in that pond. Will looked to him, I thought, as a boy would toward a well-liked older brother. Should Francis be deprived of his inheritance and of his bride, Will would feel the pain nearly as deeply as he.

And so Will plotted how best to help his friend. The plot was a harebrained plan, to be sure, but I could offer no better.

The evening was well advanced, and the sun sinking in the west, when I found Will in the back garden of his home. He looked hot and annoyed, for his mother had set him the task of forking fertilizer into the garden around the bases of all the plants, flowers and beans and cabbages alike. Though the dung heap in the corner was an old one, it smelled none the sweeter for that. "I'll help," I said. Will pointed me to a pitchfork, and the two of us forked manure.

"This is no work for a poet," Will grunted, wrinkling his nose at the stink. "Did you get what you need?"

"I have it, paints and wig and all. But we will need a costume."

"I thought a linen sheet, wound like a shroud."

"Your mother will kill us!"

Will wiped sweat away from his eyes. "No, Father bought new sheets to their bed just last autumn, and one of the worn ones has been put into the ragbag. I can filch it as secure as sleep. I think a ragged one will be better than a new one, don't you?"

"I don't know. Ben Fadger does all the costumes."

"Tattered and moldy looking," Will said in an odd dreamy way. "As though gnawed by worm and beetle! And if we can devise some way to light it strangely from beneath, why, we'll ghost Giles Speight to within an inch of his life! The hairs of his head will stand on end, sure!"

"He'll look like an angry porcupine," I said with an involuntary grin.

Will was chuckling now, leaning on his pitchfork and letting me do all the work. "His eyes will start from their sockets like shooting stars! His teeth will chatter like hail on a roof! His blood will run cold—"

From the back door of the house behind me, Mary Shakespeare said sharply, "Your breech will run warm if you don't get to work this instant, Will Shakespeare! Letting poor Tom do what I sent you to do, for shame!"

"I was just resting for a bit," Will protested, and he returned to spreading manure.

"Will," I said, "I hear a stranger is in town asking about my uncle. Have you heard anything of such a person?"

"Not I," replied Will with a thoughtful frown. "I'll ask

about. Someone new in Stratford is always a wonder, and people will be talking about such a one. That's enough for the beans. Let's start here, on the roses."

When I was sure that Will's mother was out of earshot, I said, "What speech am I to say as the ghost?"

"I have not had time to write it out," Will complained. "Mother caught me before I could get ink and paper. Never mind! I've been turning words in my head, and I'll write you a speech that will freeze Giles's very marrow! You heard old Edmund. Do you think you can imitate his voice?"

I thought back to the scene we had witnessed between Edmund and Francis. Tentatively, trying to set my voice at Edmund Speight's rusty-gate pitch, I said, "I'll have no son of mine dallying with a Cabot wench. Break it off with her now, I say, or else you'll find yourself as poor and landless as she!"

Will winced. "No, no, no," he told me. "You sound like a girl! Ouch!"

I don't know why he yelped so loud. I had not kicked him so very hard. However, I lowered my voice and tried again.

"No good," Will said. "For now you sound like a hoarse girl—no, don't kick me! It's not like him at all."

Once more I tried, this time putting a lot of breath into my words.

"Better," Will said slowly. "I like the hollow sound, but it isn't Edmund. You did not hear him speak enough, I think. Let me try it and see if this is anything like him."

He drew in a deep breath, paused for a moment, and then said, "Here, you vagabonds! What mean you, trespassing upon my land?" He raised his eyebrows and asked, "How was that?"

"Better than mine," I admitted. "Still not good enough to fool a son, though."

"How did you do that thing with your breath?"

I told him how to tighten his stomach and force the air up, making a hissing undertone to his words. He tried again, and this time I began to think he might do it. "That is not *exactly* like him," I told Will, "but it does sound strange and ghostly. On a dark night, in a lonely place, it might serve."

Will wiped his eyes again and plunged his pitchfork into the dung heap. "There, we've finished. Come in. Let's wash our hands and faces. I hate this job. I only wish I were truly a poet, and stained my fingers with nothing more smelly than good black ink!"

We had another worry that evening, for Saturday night was bathing-night. The Shakespeares had a tinned bathtub, and after supper the serving girls brought kettles of water. "Tom is the guest," Mary Shakespeare said. "Let him have the first turn in the water."

But how could I? Will, as usual, had a device: He told his brother Gilbert of a monstrous big spider he had seen in the garden, and Gilbert wanted to see it. I took the quickest bath I have ever taken, leaping out, drying myself, and putting on my long nightshirt before Will and Gilbert, who was now complaining because the spider had apparently gone, came back into the house. "I'm next," Gilbert said, beginning to undress.

"No, I'm the oldest," Will said. He winked at me. "Tom, you go into the shop and make up our woolsacks. I'll not be more than a few minutes."

Nor was he. He came in carrying a candle, his hair ruffled up from the towel. "Now," he said, producing a small inkhorn and pen and a few pieces of paper. "Now I can create."

He put the candle and paper on the counter, drew up a tall stool, and sat bending over, scratching and scribbling away. It was past ten of the clock by then, and growing dark outside. I wondered if crazed Master Coste were in the Bear again, getting drunk, and whether he would once more come a-staggering down Henley Street to gibe and caper at us. I shivered. Will was afraid of that man, and I felt a little afraid too.

In a surprisingly short time, Will thrust a sheet toward me. He had close-written over it, in a somewhat careless schoolboy script, much like the way my father had taught me to form my letters. As a girl, of course, I could not hope to go to school, but for five years or more, up until the time he had to go into hiding, my scholarly father had taught me well.

In the yellow light of that single candle, I read over the words Will had written. When I finished, I looked up at him. He stared at me anxiously, his brown eyes glittering in the candlelight. "Is it horrible?" he asked almost in a whisper.

My hopes, which had been dead, revived again. I felt tears brimming in my eyes. I could only whisper, "Oh, Will, this is wonderful. You *are* a poet!"

He relaxed then, letting out a long-held breath. "Viola," he said seriously, "if you were not a girl, I'd—why, I'd hug you!"

❧ Thirteen ❧

"Play something like the murder
of my father . . ."

I am afraid that Will and I paid small attention to Vicar Smart's sermon that Sunday morning in Holy Trinity. Indeed, I thought that as a preacher, William Smart was just the opposite of his name. "William Dull" would better fit him, it seemed to me, as his monotonous voice murmured through a psalm. However, I remained quiet and pretended to pay attention, squashed into the corner of the Shakespeare pew by Will on my left. The minister droned on and on, his voice like a lullaby in the warm church sanctuary. Some boy behind us pretended to snore, and I heard a loud smack that told me his parents would not put up with such jesting.

At long last the sermon ended, and as we spilled out of

Holy Trinity, Will threaded through the departing crowd and beckoned me to follow. He drew up to a tall boy of about my age, a dark young man with sleeked-back black hair and piercing blue eyes, who had been stooping over to scratch the ears of a pleasantly ugly, bowlegged little white dog. "Tom!" Will called to me. "This is my friend, who went to sleep during the parson's saws, or pretended to. He's our near neighbor, and his name is Hamnet Sadler."

Hamnet straightened up, gave me a lazy nod, and said, "I know who you are. Your uncle's the fellow arrested for killing old Edmund Speight." His dog came sniffing around my ankles.

"He didn't do it," I said, reaching down to pet the dog, feeling his short, wiry hair. The animal snuffled my fingers and licked my hand.

"We are going to unmask the true murderer," Will said, having pulled Hamnet aside from the crowd. "It hangs on a trick that I cannot well manage alone. Will you take part?"

"Faith," said Hamnet with a laugh, "for that, I don't care a straw that Edmund Speight is dead. Remember how he set those great slavering dogs on us last summer? How you ran! Here, Crab!"

Crab was an odd name for a white dog with a long-snouted face, but the little animal romped to his master's side. I stood behind Will, letting him talk, which seemed to be what he did best.

"You like my dog?" asked Hamnet, and I nodded. "He does tricks. Sit up, Crab! Up!"

Obediently the little dog reared up on his haunches, his forepaws stroking the air. Hamnet made him roll over, play dead, and even do a somersault-leap as Will pleaded for the boy's attention.

"He's a smart dog," I told Hamnet.

"Aye," said Hamnet with a smile, fondly reaching down to scratch Crab's head. Crab grinned, lolling out a great long pink tongue.

"Please, Hamnet, pay heed," begged Will. "Listen: Tom's uncle is a good man. He's a player, and—and there will be no play put forward so long as he must lie in prison. Come, Hamnet—you love a play! Why, when John Taborer plays his music, or John Knowles sings in the market square, there you are with eyes and ears wide open! Surely you'd want to come and see Tom's uncle's most excellent comedy!"

"Is it a good play?" Hamnet asked, his blue eyes challenging me to say that it was.

"We have all kinds of plays," I told him. "I must know parts for more than a dozen of them. Plays of laughter and plays of murder, stories of love and revenge and magic, of fairies and of witches, of blood and thunder."

"There!" Will said in triumph. "Think of that, Hamnet! Help us just a little, just a very little—you will hardly even call it a bother—and when Tom's uncle is set free, such a play you will see! Tom will make sure you are in the very front, where you can take in every word and every action. The play's the thing, Hamnet, the play's the thing!"

Hamnet crossed his arms and tilted his head on one side, still looking unconvinced. "And what must I do, Will? I'll tell you flat, if it's like the time we were going to make the town believe the devil had run through in the middle of the night, I'll none of it!"

"What?" I asked.

"Two winters back," Will said in a tight, urgent voice. "Light snowfall. A pair of old shoes with wooden hoofs nailed to the soles. Long story."

"For what purpose?" I asked.

Will turned an exasperated face toward me. "Why, to shake things up! To give Stratford some excitement!"

"That's the stupidest thing I've ever heard!"

"Do I call thy plays stupid?" asked Will, red-faced. "Ouch!"

Hamnet chuckled. "Why, Will, dost let a boy strike thee on the arm so hard? Fight back!"

Will rubbed his arm. "Nay, Hamnet, I have reasons not to strike him, though I could easily beat him most pitifully."

I balled my fists. "Try it!"

Will frowned at me. "What, and have everyone say I beat a boy smaller than myself?"

"What do you mean, smaller?" I snapped.

By then Hamnet was laughing. "Nay, nay, Will thinks himself a giant on earth! He treats me just the same, though you see I tower over him. All right, all right. What I say, Will, is that I'll do none of your tricks if they're like to fetch me such a whipping as we got last time."

To Hamnet, Will wheedled, "None of that, Hamnet, none of that. No risk in the world, no chance of being whipped. You simply have to place a note where Giles Speight will be sure to find it, that's all. I cannot risk being seen, for he knows me too well, and Tom's got his uncle to think of."

"I don't know . . ."

Will glanced down at the dog and suddenly said, "If you do this favor for us, when the play goes forward, Tom will let Crab have a part in it!"

"What!" I said.

"What part could Crab take in a play?" asked Hamnet, looking as astonished as I felt.

Will said, "Why—why, in a play with a scene set in

moonlight, he could be the Man in the Moon's dog! Everyone knows that the Man in the Moon carries a load of thorn branches and leads his dog!" He nudged me. "You act plays that take place in moonlight, do you not, Tom?"

"Oh, yes," I lied. "Dozens."

That temptation proved too strong, and without further argument, Hamnet Sadler surrendered to the besieging Will like an undefended village facing an army of ogres. We found a shady spot to sit, where Will whipped out his small inkhorn and the cut-short goose feather he used as a pen. "Who would be a good witness to lure Giles out?" he asked me.

I shrugged. "I know nothing of the people in town," I began. Then I smiled. "Stay, though, I do know one. What about that mad fellow, the sexton? He pops up everywhere, and at odd hours."

"Costard!" exclaimed Will with a laugh, and Hamnet, though he did not fully understand everything we were doing, grinned wickedly as he tickled Crab's pointed ears. Will scribbled for a minute, then read the note aloud to us:

Master Giles,

There are deeds done in the light, and deeds done in the dark. What I saw you do on the banks of the river was a dark deed, truly the kind of deed that calls for punishment and penance. Meet me half-past midnight on the far side of Clopton Bridge, and we will talk of the penance your soul is to do. Come alone. Remember, old Chaucer said many a man, even an archdeacon, hath his soul in his purse, so I tell thee, bring thy soul, and put money in thy purse.

Clarence Coste

Hamnet raised his eyebrows. "And are you going to send Costard a letter from Giles Speight as well?"

"Nay, we don't want *him* there," Will said. "This, though, is sure to fetch Giles." He blew upon the ink to dry it, and then he folded the paper and handed it over to Hamnet. "Watch and be sure that Giles is not at home when you go to leave this," he said. "It would be best to leave Crab behind too, for where people see him, they look for you, Hamnet. Wait until it's close to evening. And then nip in and nip out the way Diggory Bracebridge runs at football, with a dart and a twist and an eye on every side of your head! Don't let anyone see you, for 'twould never do to be caught in the act."

Hamnet's smile was mischievous. "The day Giles Speight could catch me has not yet dawned," he said in a tone of disdain, and he took the folded paper. "He shall have it ere night falls, Will."

We started back to Will's house, and on the way I began to tell Will that I was *not* smaller than he, but before I got more than three words out, Will suddenly hissed, "Who's that?"

I jerked my head around. Standing in a doorway just to our left was a tall, lean, dark young man, dressed head to foot in black. From his swarthy complexion you would have thought him a Spaniard. He stared at me with brown eyes like gimlets, then quickly withdrew into the house. "I don't know him," I said. "It might be the stranger who is asking about my uncle."

"I don't like the look of him," said Will. "He's too lean, too hungry looking."

"Whose house is this?" I asked.

His expression became a little troubled. "It belongs to the Reynolds family. I don't think they would harbor a spy, but—well, you never know. Come, we're late."

At Will's house his mother gave us a mild scolding for dawdling so. In honor of the Sabbath, Mary Shakespeare had brought out two pewter plates for her husband and herself, but the rest of us, being children, made do with the same treens that we had seen at every other meal, and we wiped our greasy fingers on the same rough-wove cloths. Afterward, Will's mother caught us before we could dash out, and she set us a-cleaning the table. Will grumbled, but I told him 'twas only fair for me to help a bit, since his family had so much helped me.

Will had already filched the worn sheet that was to be my costume, and now he artfully ripped it so it would flow and flutter with every movement of my arms. It looked good, having been washed so many times that it was pale gray, not white, and so thin that a breath would flutter it.

Then Will set to devising how to illuminate our ghost, for even in June, half-past midnight would be a dark time of night indeed. He found an old bottle of blue glass and was puzzling how to put a candle inside it when a great crack of thunder crashed, startling him so he dropped the bottle. The neck broke off, and he pounced on the bottom part with a triumphant cry. "This will do!"

I looked out the window. Silvery spikes of rain danced on the cobblestones and murmured in the straw of the thatched roof. "If it rains—"

"This is only a summer shower," Will said impatiently, picking up pieces of broken glass. "'Twill pass within an hour, never fear."

He knew Warwickshire weather well, and true to his

promise, the shower swept by and the sun broke out later that afternoon. We tried the broken bottle and found that, if we set a stubby candle upright and placed the broken part of the bottle carefully down over it, we got a pleasingly dim blue light. Then I went through the paints and began to plan what I would use, whilst Will memorized the speech he was to say in an imitation of Edmund Speight's voice.

Very late in the afternoon, when the sun yet lingered low in the west, we strolled across the bridge and scouted a place for our play-acting. All along the riverbanks willows and oaks grew thick, and perhaps ten yards past the bridge there stood an old dying oak, one with a conveniently low, thick branch. Will thought it would be perfect, and I found I could easily climb up.

Then Will fell to looking for some way to conceal our blue lantern. Using a heavy piece of bark as a spade, he dug into the earth between the tree roots until he had excavated a shallow little hollow two handsbreadth across and perhaps eight inches deep. In front of that we put some fallen branches, artfully arranged. "That should do," Will said at last, slapping his hands together. "Now all that remains is to wait for the witching hour of the night. If we do it well, the play will catch Giles Speight's conscience—catch it as a mousetrap catches a mouse!"

❧ Fourteen ❧

"Grim-grinning ghost . . ."

We heard the clocks toll midnight as I put on the last of the paint. In the light of three candles, I gazed at my unfamiliar face in a blotchy and speckled looking glass that Will had smuggled into the shop.

I would never be as convincing a wraith or spirit as the skeleton-thin Michael Moresby, but with my skin whitened, my eyes outlined in black circles, and with purple hollows beneath my cheekbones, I looked dead enough. Like Michael, I had painted black lines on my whitened lips so that it looked as if my face had the grim, toothy grin of a skull. I had even remembered to imitate Edmund Speight's hooked nose and had glued on curls of wool that looked much like the old man's thick shaggy eyebrows. With the wig perched on my head, I did look a bit like him, or a bit like he would look after having died and been buried for a few days, I thought.

Will approved of my appearance in general, tugging my wig more firmly onto my head. Then he said, "Let's try it in the light." Blowing out two of the candles, he set the third on the floor and then covered it with the broken part of the bottle. The shattered end let in enough air for the candle to burn, though it flickered a bit.

"You make a ghastly ghost!" Will crowed, holding the looking glass so I could see what he saw. I had to admit that my appearance was likely to frighten Giles Speight or, for that matter, anyone else: My skeletal features wavered in the uncertain, flickering blue light, and the ghastly, unnatural color made me look like a soul in the Catholics' Purgatory, suffering for my sins.

"It's time to go." Will gathered up everything that we would need. Then very quietly we stepped out into the still-damp streets.

Thinking our plans were all spoiled, I wailed, "It's foggy!"

"All the better," whispered Will, encumbered with the sheet, our piece of blue bottle, and a dark lantern with a burning candle inside it. "Who expects a spirit to appear on a star-shining night with a bright moon sailing in the sky? Come along!"

"Do you want me to carry some of—"

"Nay, just think of your acting and leave everything else to me. Come, I tell you!" It was lucky for me that he was there to guide, for with the heavy pall of fog and the darkness of the night, I would have been lost in the first dozen steps. The few lights that burned in scattered windows here and there made mere pale, yellowish blurs in the night.

The fog grew even thicker as we neared the river, and I began to wonder if we could be seen at all in this murk. It was like thrusting your head beneath a gray blanket. We crossed the bridge, hearing the murmur of the river and smelling its fresh clean water. Remembering how we had scrambled down the bank and pulled the drowned body to shore, I shivered.

This time Will made no pause on the bridge to listen to the river's song, but instead led me surely and quickly to the base of the dying old oak. The boy again reminded me of a cat, a creature that can see in the dark. I was not so gifted and had to thrust out my hands, feeling my way as Will boosted me, grunting from my weight. I pulled myself up to the big tree branch, rough but cool and clammy from the fog, and Will tossed the ragged sheet up to me. Lying along the branch on my stomach, I draped the sheet over my head and thrust my arms through the holes Will had made for me. Will adjusted the part of the sheet that hung straight down. I would look, we hoped, like a ghost hovering mysteriously two feet off the ground.

Will could not forego taking a peep at me in the light of the candle. He took it out of the dark lantern, set it into the hole, and carefully placed the bottle over it. I could see that the flickering blue light gave the rolling fog a strange and eerie glow. Will stepped back and whispered, "Come forward six inches on the branch."

"That's not easy to do!" However, moving a little like an inchworm, humping up my spine and clinging to the branch with my knees, I slipped forward, keeping my balance atop the limb with some difficulty. "How is this?"

"Better. Yes, good, right there. Now the light is right on the sheet and your face. Wave your arms! No, don't try to flap like a bird! Don't saw the air with your hands! Move slowly, slowly!"

I moved my arms in a sluggish circular motion, as if I were treading water in the deep weir of the Avon and on the verge of exhaustion. Beneath me the hanging sheet swayed and seemed to float uncannily in mid-air. "Thou art perfect!" Will crowed. While I sprawled uncomfortably atop the wet branch, he covered the hole with a bit of curved bark, so almost no light leaked out, and to the bark he tied a long string. He hid behind the tree, ready to twitch the bark covering aside and reveal the floating ghost when the time grew ripe.

The quarter-hour had already rung, and just as Will hid I heard the chime of the half hour. If Master Hamnet Sadler had done his duty, Giles Speight should be on his way to confront mad Clarence Coste at the far side of the Stratford bridge. Though we waited to frighten him, I must admit that within myself I felt a cold dread. The night, the fog, the uncertainty were all making me anxious and fearful.

To still my heart's wild, frightened thumping, I fell to trying to think of some play in which Hamnet's dog Crab might reasonably appear. He seemed to be a good, biddable animal, unlikely to cause the kind of trouble that the gray donkey my uncle once brought onstage in *Lucius Transform'd* had done, when the beast waited until he was before a crowd of people to make gallons of gushing, steaming yellow water, to much laughter and applause. Crab would be no good for the Lion in *Pyramus*, for he was much too small, nor would he serve as the hell-hound in *Murder Aveng'd*. Maybe, though, the Lady in *Temperance* might hold Crab in her lap in the scene where she toyed with her young swain, for often times great ladies choose the oddest little lapdogs as their pets—

And at that very moment a hound howled dolefully somewhere in the distance, as though it wanted on purpose to make me jump half out of my skin. Then not far off an owl began to moan, a mournful *hoooo, huh-hoooohoorruh,* repeated over and over as though the bird had some terrible sorrow in its little heart and was weeping over it. I began to wonder if Hamnet Sadler had forgotten or failed us, or if the note might somehow have gone astray.

Then I heard footsteps on the bridge, slow and heavy. Giles Speight, I thought, and it seemed to me that he was making slow going of it, probably groping his way through the fog and the night with his hand upon the parapet. The sound ceased. He must have stepped off the bridge and onto the damp grassy margin of the high road. Why didn't Will open our blue lantern and speak his words? Perhaps he was waiting for a word from Speight, I thought, to show that he was close enough to see me through the drifting mists.

More footsteps! Had Giles given up and gone back to the bridge? It sounded as if he had, though truly in the darkness I could not tell whether the sounds I heard were approaching us or going back toward Stratford. Then I heard a low voice call, "Here!"

Giles Speight then spoke up more loudly, his pinched, quarrelsome voice unmistakable: "I've come, curse you! What do you mean by this trick?"

Sudden blue light erupted upward as Will jerked the bark covering off our hidden candle. I heard a gasp, and Giles Speight growled, "The devil!"

Then as I had practiced I slowly waved my arms, making our dangling ghost sway weirdly in the dim blue glow below me, while from his hiding place behind the tree, Will, in his breathy, uncanny imitation of old Edmund Speight's cranky, creaky voice began to speak:

"Unnat'ral boy! I am thy father's ghost,
And am return'd to haunt a murd'rous son!
Thou wicked youth, confess thy bloody deed—
Admit how thou thy father struck and killed!
For else I'll harrow up thy blood with groans
And doleful cries for ghastly vengeance dire!
O, tormenting fiends shall snatch thy soul,
Thy blotted, blighted, rotten soul—"

"Who's that? A ghost? A fig's end!" yelled a hoarse and contemptuous voice I knew all too well: 'Twas Clarence Coste, the drunken, mad sexton! What was *he* doing there?

Something swished through the air, and I felt the dangling sheet jerk sharply below me. Coste had thrown something at me—a stone that crashed into the trunk of the oak and thumped to earth. Will, probably as startled as I, forgot the speech he had prepared and instead began to ad-lib, his voice squeaking up in pitch from sheer alarm: "Foolish man! Thy vain missiles pass straight through my insubstantial floating form, come from, uh, the agony of sulfurous flames to accuse thee! Go away, before I, uh, rip the heart from out thy breast—"

"That's no ghost! Pull the rogue down!" shouted Giles Speight, and someone, leaping forward, trod on our candle and put it out with a crunch of breaking glass, plunging all into darkness. "My foot!" shouted Giles, who must have cut himself on the broken bottle.

"Get down!" Will bellowed in his own voice.

I made no pause at all, but slipped from out the sheet and dropped quickly to the ground. A hand swiped at my sleeve, barely gripping it, and I jerked away, shouting, "You let me go!"

I whirled around and darted behind the oak's trunk and ran full-tilt into Will, who grabbed me, spun me about like a top, and into my ear urgently whispered the word I had heard him say often enough before:

"Run!"

❦ Fifteen ❧

"Our wills and fates do so contrary run
That our devices still are overthrown . . ."

Will seized my hand and took the lead as we fled in the blind night, running headlong from two cursing, blundering men. I heard the ripping as one of them seized the dangling sheet and tore it loose from the branch. Then one yelled, "There he goes, away to the right! I hear the rogue! Catch him, catch him!"

Will was all but dragging me as he ran, leaping over obstacles that I could not see at all. Several times I stumbled and tripped, once turning my ankle painfully, but still limped on, trusting Will not to run us into a tree or dash out into the Avon. The sounds of pursuit died away, the men seeming to believe that we were heading straight eastward instead of circling to the south, following the line of the river. Will did not slacken his pace, though it was costing me much effort to try to keep up with him.

The breath was beginning to burn my windpipe, rasping in gasps from our efforts, when at last Will slowed. For some little time we stood bent-backed and hacking, and then he asked, "Are you all right?"

"I'm wet and scraped from the tree branch," I whispered back harshly, feeling nothing but anger. "And I've hurt my ankle, and my throat is as dry as a bone, and I'm about to die for want of air. Except for those few discomforts, I'm very well, I thank you."

"Blame me not!" Will objected, panting so deeply that he wheezed. He danced aside, and for once avoided the blow I'd aimed at his arm. "How was I to know that Costard would come? Hamnet must have blundered! I told him, did I not, that he was not to speak to Coste or give him note, and you see sure he must have done one or 'tother, or else why did the sexton come spot on the minute to the very place where we had lured Giles Speight?"

"Well, your ghost trick failed," I said, rubbing my sore ankle. "It might have wound up with our being killed, too, but it did not work as you thought it would."

"By my soul and by my faith, it *should* have worked!" Will answered in a kind of quiet fury. "I had thought of everything aforehand, and only Costard's coming ruined it all. Before the Lord, it was a good plot—an admirable plot! And you were a good player. An excellent plot, a very good player!"

"It did not work," I reminded him, speaking clearly and pronouncing each word very plain, for to me that seemed the most important point.

"It *would* have," grumbled Will. "If only Giles had come alone, I am sure it would have worked. We would have frightened the man's wits out of him, were he by himself. A lone man facing a real ghost—his blood would freeze, his very soul would shrink from mere terror! Two men together, though, why, they lend and borrow courage even on the darkest night. Why the devil did Costard want to come there, anyway, where he had no business in the world? I tell you, that mad Costard lent some man's mettle to Giles, or else we'd have had the murderer, sure!"

We were some little way from the river, which I could hear and smell rather than see. A tree had fallen or had been cut some time before, and when we ran against its fallen trunk, I sat down and rubbed my swollen ankle. I heard Will plop down beside me, still muttering about the way the sexton had ruined a perfectly good plan. "Will," I said wearily, "pray don't think me ungrateful, but please don't help me any more."

I could sense that he turned toward me in the darkness to plead his case. "Tom—Viola—it could have worked! Next time, we must—"

"Oh, go to!" I spoke louder and harsher than I'd meant to, but Will had tried my patience and had vexed me sadly that night, and what with being dizzy-headed for lack of sleep and cold and damp from having lain on a dripping tree branch, and troubled by an aching twisted ankle, I had grown quite sick of Will and his sugared words and his overcomplicated plotting. "I think I'd better move back to our camp in the morning," I muttered. "Alan will be back from London some time this week with money, and perhaps when he comes we should hire that lawyer and place our trust in him to advise Uncle Matt."

"Hire Lawyer Collins?" Will asked, sounding amazed. "Girl, you could not have a single good word of advice from him for one farthing less than ten pounds! That's a mortal sight of money. Where is your friend going to find ten whole pounds, and Collins will probably want it in gold, too!"

"I don't know!" I all but shouted, so loudly that somewhere across the river a dog heard me and yapped back. With an effort I lowered my voice. "Will, we're not going to frighten a confession out of Giles Speight. It was a stupid notion to begin with. Why, look you, we didn't fool him or Clarence

Coste even for an instant. If they put their heads together and talk about it, they're pretty sure to guess that you were behind the trick—"

"How so?" Will asked indignantly. "By my faith, did I not plan it all out most cunningly? Who's he that can read my hand in anything we did tonight? Why, not even my father or mother knows what we were about!"

"I suspect all of Stratford would think of Will Shakespeare when they get word of a fluttering ghost and an unearthly light. Someone will say, 'Oh, dear, who could have thought of such a flea-brained, knot-pated, foolish scheme as this?' And someone else is sure to answer, 'Here, what was the name of the lad who nailed hoofs on his feet and then tried to fool us all into thinking the devil had strolled through town?'"

I could feel the log that we sat on trembling as Will writhed. If I had been him, I would have twitched too, out of mere embarrassment. "This is different!"

I stood up and tested my ankle. It throbbed with pain, but I believed it would take my weight. "No, Will, it isn't different. It's just the same. Just—just forget about my uncle and me. Let us do for ourselves. You can't help us, and we're better off without you."

"Viola, please—there's a stranger in town asking about your uncle, and that might be dangerous. Unless we find the true murderer, your uncle's very life is in the balance. But in friendship—"

"I'm *not* your friend!" I snarled. What did you have to do to this boy to make him see you were sick of him and his harebrained schemes? "I-I told you once before, I hate all Catholics!"

"You're no ranting Puritan yourself, Viola," Will said softly and resentfully. "And your parents had a soft spot for a priest, you said."

"Only because my father had grown up with him and felt sorry for him! They were foolish to do what they did," I shot back, wondering why my hot cheeks didn't shine in the night. "If that priest had been any sort of Christian, he wouldn't have let them put their necks in the noose for him!"

"Maybe you think it would be better to put a noose around the neck of a man who lives to serve God!"

"Maybe I would!"

"I take it back," Will said hotly. "You *are* a ranting Puritan—or at least you talk like one!"

"Better than any idol-worshipping, knee-crooking fool of a—"

"You take that back!"

"I will not!" I squared my shoulders. "Hit me if you

dare, and I'll teach you a lesson in manners, Master Will Shakespeare!"

"I can't hit a girl!"

"But you can put one up in a tree to suffer cold and damp!"

He had nothing to say to that. For one or two long-seeming minutes we stood in the foggy night breathing hard. Then, in a tight voice, he said, "We'd better get home. There's one o'clock striking now."

We went on through the fog, with Will no longer holding my hand, but me blundering and stumbling along behind him. Gruffly, Will said we would make for the mill bridge, past the weir. That suited me. We'd pass the players' camp, and I thought I could slip into my uncle's tent and be shed of this pest of a boy. We came to a little stream that sprang from a rocky bed before meandering down the hill toward the Avon, and Will led me to its small pool. "Water's clean to drink," he muttered. "And maybe you'd better wash your face. Here, I saved this." He fumbled something into my hands, something soft: a piece of the sheet I had worn, somewhat bigger than a man's handkerchief.

"Thank you," I said stiffly. I cupped my hands and drank, stilling a raging thirst, and then I knelt and washed my face in the stingingly cold water. I could not see at all, of course, but I know the feel of makeup paint, and after peeling off my wig I rubbed and scrubbed until I thought most of the stuff would be gone, finally drying my face on the square of linen Will had handed me. "Don't you still have the dark-lantern?" I asked.

"No tinder or flint," Will said. "And no spare candle."

So we went the rest of the way in the dark. We passed the bridge without even seeing it and got into muddy ground that sucked at our shoes and overflowed them. With much trouble we turned back and retraced our steps. Finally, when the clock was about to strike two, we found the narrow footbridge and crossed the Avon south of town. As we got to the far bank, Will said, "Around here is where that old fellow found part of your uncle's walking-stick."

"I know."

"It's strange," he said thoughtfully. "Old Edmund always hobbled around town with a walking-stick too. I wonder what became of his."

"It makes no difference."

"It does," Will said doggedly.

"But he didn't mean to do much walking," I pointed out. "Cordelia told us he rode a bay gelding into town."

"Aye, that's true. I suppose he expected to walk only from his horse into the lawyer's house and go no farther afoot. But after all, he did—they said he was all over town looking for someone to witness his will, and at the end he limped out of the Swan all but lame." After a long time, Will added a soft, "Viola, I'm sorry for what I said."

Well, I wasn't sorry for what *I* had said, and instead of replying, I clamped my mouth shut and just walked along in angry silence. If anything, the fog had thickened. I could not even be sure where the camp was, and not wanting to spend a chilly night in the open, I finally said I would stay in the Shakespeare house one last night.

"Don't go back to the players," Will pleaded. "I need your help if I'm to find a way to set your uncle free."

I wasn't even angry any longer, just sick and tired of his chatter and his ideas. "Will, it isn't right that your mother and father are feeding me and giving me a place to sleep. I don't want to be in the debt of—"

"Of Catholics," Will said bitterly. "You complain we're ungodly, and you won't accept a bit of simple Christian charity if we offer it. I think God must weep in sorrow and anger over the bloody ruin men have made of his teachings."

"No, it really is not that. It's just—just that I don't *feel* right," I said. "Will, I don't really hate you. I've seen more of the world than you have, and I know that some things are, well, just childish, that's all. My uncle is in jail, a dark stranger is prying into his affairs, and maybe his very life is in jeopardy. Nothing the two of us can do will change that."

"Where are we?" Will asked all of a sudden.

"Don't you know?"

"I thought we were still in Mill Lane, but we should have come to the church before this. We must have walked right past Holy Trinity without seeing it. Now I don't know if we're in Sanctuary Lane or in Church Way, or even in what direction we're walking."

We found there were buildings on either side of us, and Will said that ruled out Sanctuary Lane, which led past Lime Close and through the Salmon's Tail, whatever that was. The way we were taking at last curved to the right and then, in relief, he said we were in Church Street and had but to follow it to the High Cross, and then Henley Street would be just away to our left. The clocks tolled twice. Two had already struck, so it was half-past two, as late as I could ever recall being awake. I was shivering in the clammy chill of night, and my feet were numb from having been soaked when we had stumbled into the mud. "I hope we may not come down with agues," I muttered.

We almost ran smack onto the cross, and then, gaining confidence, Will led me through a quick series of turns, right, then left, then right and left again, and he said we were close to home. He felt his way along the house-fronts until he whispered, "This is it."

Will had left the shop door unlocked. He opened it, and we slipped inside. I sighed in relief at the relative warmth, and I stooped to unlace and take off my wet shoes. "What a night," Will said.

Then from the darkness, a man's voice said softly, "What a night indeed. Will, you have brought a burden of trouble on yourself."

My heart sank. Will's father was sitting somewhere in the dark. Lord knows when he had missed us, or how long he had been waiting there.

However, it must have been long enough to suit him. He sounded very displeased.

❧ **Sixteen** ❧

"And tell me now, thou naughty varlet, tell me,
where hast thou been . . . ?"

John Shakespeare fetched a lantern and in its yellow light
he stared tight-lipped at his head-drooping son. "Thou
knowest full well 'tis a crime to be abroad so late at night,"
he said. "Will, what were you about, lad? What mad scheme
have you hatched in that head of yours? Tell me!"

"Oh, sir," I said, wincing because even the soft light of
his lantern hurt my eyes and my head, " 'twas my fault. I
wanted to go back to the bridge and look to see if anything
there might show that my uncle did not do the murder he is
accused of. I asked Will if he would lead me, and he agreed.
See, Will took a lantern—though the candle-stub has
burned out—and when we found nothing at the bridge, we
went through town to look at the place where Ben Fadger

found my uncle's broken stick. But with the candle burned clean out, we quite lost our way in the darkness and fog. Will would not have gone to begin with, but that I asked him, sir, so if one of us must be whipped, pray whip me." Even as I improvised, I scolded myself for lying to save rascally Will from a whipping. Still, he *had* tried to help me.

After a moment's silence, Will's father grunted, a sound not of agreement and not of happiness, but of resignation and deep regret. "Will," he said in his terrible quiet voice, worse than an angry shout, "art not ashamed of thyself? I know thee well, my son, and I know that Tom minces this matter, making thy part in it seem lighter than it is. Wouldst thou let an innocent take thy punishment, as Tom offers to do? Shame, Will! I thought I was raising a man!"

"Please, sir," mumbled Will, sounding so heart-sore that he made me feel pained as well, "you are in the right of it. 'Twas not Tom, but I who thought of the plan. Father, can you blame Tom for wondering? His parents are both dead, and only his uncle and he are left of his family on this side of the grave! I hope, sir, that if you are ever in such straits as Tom's Uncle Matthew is now that I might be forgiven for trying every shift I could think of to help in some way."

"In some *lawful* way," said John Shakespeare firmly. "Well, you are wet and shivering and cold, and I will not whip you, though Lord knows you deserve at least that. If you were but a few years older and were caught larking in Stratford so late at night, you would stand in the stocks, Will, in the shameful stocks! Would you like that?"

Will shook his head.

"You say you would not," his father said in a tone of deep disgust. "Yet I swear before Heaven, I think you would do it just to try how it feels to have your head and hands locked in the form, to have people jeer you and pelt you with mud, with rotten fruit, even with stones! Now attend me closely, my son! You are to stay close within the house until I give you leave to go out again—and the way I feel now, that may not be until you have seen your twenty-first birthday! Do you understand me, son?"

"Aye, sir."

"Sir," I said, still trying to help the only person who'd tried to help me, "I feel to blame, truly I do. It's too late for me to go tonight, but tomorrow I will leave you and your good wife and go back to my people in the camp. Whensoever I have the money, I will try my best to repay all your kindness."

John Shakespeare smiled, though in the lantern light he looked bone-weary and sad. "Let there be no talk of repayment," he said softly. "I know what thy parents really are, Tom Pryne, though I know not their real names. Did you think your uncle Matthew shaped your wanderings to pass through Stratford quite by accident? No, there are those here in town that bear your parents good will, for the Christian help they rendered a godly man. However, if you want to go, you have my leave to leave us. You see my son has much trouble telling praiseworthy actions from bad, from knowing what is mere play from what is serious." He rose and reached for his lantern. "Now to bed, both of you boys, and no more foolishness tonight! Will, we'll speak more of this in the morning."

He left us in the dark shop, and I crept beneath my blanket feeling almost as though I really had been whipped. Will's father had been right: my very bones ached from the damp and the coolness of the night. Will whispered, "Thanks, Viola."

"'Twas more or less the truth," I muttered.

"I—oh, I'm sorry! It seemed such a grand plot—and surely it cannot be a lawless course to break curfew in lawful cause!"

"I will be away to our camp tomorrow," I said. "And then you'll have no more reason to cause your good father so much heart-sorrow."

"I wish you would stay."

To that I gave no answer, but lay trying to find warmth under my blanket, with my cheek resting on my hand. The night's wanderings had chilled me to the bone, and my twisted ankle still ached most dolorously.

To say I went to sleep that night is wrong, for instead I went to nightmare, fast-flowing terrible dreams of pursuit through a dark world, and the leaping fiend behind me sometimes was Clarence Coste holding high his spade, intending to bury me alive; and sometimes it was Giles Speight, yelling taunts at me for a poor unbelievable ghost and throwing stones; and worst of all, sometimes it was the true ghost of Edmund, glowing a dismal blue and flying fluttering through the air while howling like an owl.

The next morning my throat ached terribly, my head pounded, and I struggled hard to breathe. I wanted to rise up off my bed of bagged sheep's wool, but somehow the whole room spun and spun around me. Then I felt a cool hand on my aching forehead and thought it was that of my mother; but when I said, "Mother, is that you?" Mary Shakespeare said, "Poor child, lie still. You have a bad fever."

I remember nothing very clearly for some time after that, just flashes of aches and pains and something that tasted terrible and burned its way down my gullet as though I sipped liquid fire. When next I came to myself, I lay in a bed, and next to it sat Mary Shakespeare, her face drawn into tired lines. She seemed to doze, but when I moved, her eyes snapped open, and she said, "How do you feel?"

"Better," I said, for the pain that had clenched my throat had eased and my head no longer ached so dismally. "Better, I thank you."

"You are welcome—Viola," she said.

I sat up in bed, alarmed, but she shook her head and smiled. "Nay, no one knows save Will and me. That boy, that boy! You do most admirably for a stripling boy of eleven or twelve, Viola, but I bathed you and dressed you in that nightshirt, and Will knew that I would find out. He told me of your parents' plight. Well, I'll not break your faith nor spoil your secret. Can you eat a little? Dr. Wells said thin porridge would be best—"

"Dr. Wells?" I asked. "Has he seen me?"

"Twice, Monday and Wednesday," Will's mother said. "And I do not believe that man noticed you were a girl—these men are so unnoticing! We have been giving you his medicines when you drink—you remember nothing of that?"

Indeed I had a few hazy recollections of swallowing some nasty-tasting liquids, but nothing certain. "Why, what day is it today?" I asked.

"Thursday morning, dear," said Mrs. Shakespeare. "You lie right still, and I'll fetch you a bowl of gruel."

She brought a kind of thin brew of oats, sweetened with honey, and though at first I had no appetite for it at all, after swallowing but one spoonful I found myself as hungry as the ravening shark. I finished the bowl, and then drank a cup of good foamy milk and felt better almost at once. "I have been a sad trouble to you," I told her. "And now I owe money for the doctor, too."

"No, you haven't been a bother, and you owe me nothing," she said fondly. In a soft, nearly tearful voice she added, "Bless you, child, you are almost the age my poor little Margaret would have been had she lived. I would be hard of heart indeed to refuse the few trifling things we have done for you."

"And is it truly Thursday?" I asked again, wonderingly. I somehow had lost Monday, Tuesday, and Wednesday entirely—and 'twas Thursday when Alan was supposed to return from London! "Please, may I have my clothes and shoes?" I asked timidly.

"Dr. Wells said when your fever broke yesterday that you were not to run about, but to walk slowly, like a Christian. And I am afraid your shoes were quite spoilt by mud, dear—but I've a cousin who's a cobbler, and he's given you an old pair of his son's, neatly mended but too worn to sell. They will fit you, I think, for the nonce. I'm sorry they are no better. And I am so sorry about your hair."

I clapped my hand to my head and found that someone had cropped my hair almost as short as Crab's coat! Of course I knew that people did that to keep a fever from going to the brain—but I had before never had such a fever, and it was a shock to find my collar-length yellow curls all gone. "'Twill grow back," I said, trying to sound more cheerful than I felt.

She had washed and ironed my clothes, too, that good woman. I put them on and slipped my feet into the unfamiliar shoes. As she had told me, it was an old pair, worn most wonderfully soft, though the soles and heels looked almost new. Truth to tell, I suspected that her cousin had not really parted with the shoes for nothing, but I knew Mary Shakespeare would never let me know how much they had cost her.

Will was downstairs, looking anxious. "How do you feel?" he asked as soon as I tottered down, feeling shaky and weak. "You look so pale! You frightened us, I can tell you that. You were burning up with fever! 'Twas the night damps, Dr. Wells swore, that gave it to you. Listen, much has happened. Come with me."

"Will your father let you go out again?" I asked.

Will laughed. "By my faith, Father was so worried about you that he forgot all about my punishment—though to be sure, I've been most wonderfully helpful around the house these last few days. He sold the wool on Tuesday, and I helped him load it into the man's wagon, and Father gave me a penny piece and told me I was a good boy, by the Lord, so he called me! But come now, and I will tell you what's ado."

We went out into the morning sun, which seemed far too bright to me after my days inside. Will kept glancing at me. "I know I look strange," I said.

"You do look different," Will acknowledged. "More like a boy. I think I would not have guessed you for a girl when first we met had your hair been cropped then as it is now. Would you like a cap?"

"Yes, please," I said, for in the open my head felt cool and strange. He ducked back inside and a moment later returned with a brown cloth cap that I pulled down to my ears. "Now how do I look?"

"Like a country boy," Will said with a ready grin. "But listen: Your uncle is bound over until the next Assizes. Justice Roberts, a shallow old fellow, heard his cause and said there is enough evidence to hold him. The old man, Fadger, he held to a fine of five pound, and I got Father to stand surety, so he has been released and has gone back to the tents to stay with the other players. Lawyer Collins is to read Edmund Speight's will come Monday, and that's when my school begins again, too, so we have not much time—"

"Will," I said firmly, "I meant what I said before I fell ill. I'm through with your tricks and your plots."

"But this one is sure to work," he objected. "Listen: Costard got drunk in the Bear two nights ago now, and he spun out such a story of ghosts and blue blazes that I truly believe had we set out to frighten him, not Giles, we would have had good success! The man I heard the story from told me that Costard swore truth out of Stratford that he was alone when he saw a horrible hobgoblin spirit floating among the trees. He told a thousand incomprehensible lies about his courage—how he fought the ghost for a long hour by Stratford clock, what blows, what wards, what devices he used to overcome it and send it packing back to the devil! But mark you this most especially: He swore he was alone, all, all alone!"

"And we know that's a lie, but why do you think it's noteworthy?" I asked, my head still feeling light from the fever.

"'Tis plain as the blessed sun!" Will said. "Costard was close enough—he must have heard my speech! He knows now that Giles Speight slew his own father. I'll warrant that the mad fellow is shrewd enough to see that when Giles comes into his father's money, he will pay dearly for what Costard heard!"

"You mean he believes Giles killed Edmund, and now he'll demand money from Giles to keep quiet?"

"Aye, there's nothing so probable to sense as that! Now, if Costard knows, Costard could tell—I'll grant you, he is not so handsome a witness as we could wish, but when misfortune comes showering down, we must take what scant shelter we can find! Here's the point: Costard half believes that what he saw was no trick, but a very ghost. 'Twould take the merest nudge to make him think that ghost has come to haunt him! We can—"

"No, Will," I said firmly. "We cannot. I'm sorry, but we cannot."

I walked away from him, heading for our camp. Fifty steps away I glanced back. Poor Will still stood there, gazing forlornly after me, looking like nothing so much as a puppy whose master had beaten it for no reason.

Seventeen

"... taken by the insolent foe ..."

Though the clocks had not yet tolled noon, young Alan Franklin had arrived back in camp before me. I found him rubbing down poor Molly, who looked as if she had made a hard trip of it, with the others clustered around him asking questions, all except for Ben Fadger, who crouched over the cauldron like the Witch in *The Curst King*, muttering darkly and stirring a bubbling, fragrant stew.

Peter Stonecypher saw me approaching and gave me a wave and as cheery a smile as a worried man could muster. "Here's Tom back again! Alan's brought us good news, Tom—why, what have you done to your hair, lad?"

I explained in haste that I had come down with a fever and that the Shakespeares had been obliged to trim my hair close, and then I said, "No matter, for it will grow again. Quick, tell me the good news, for I need a kind word!"

With an understanding nod, Peter said, "Here it is, then: Master Burbage has sent money to hire a lawyer to advise Matthew. Now we'll see what's what."

"Oh, yes," grumbled Ben to the crackling campfire. "Oh, yes, now we has money for the lawyer, and money for that there iniqueertous swingerin' fine, and all that's very well as may be, but what's to eat upon, I arsks? Where's the money for bread and beer and cheese and meat, that's all I wants to know."

"Never mind him," said Alan, jingling a fat leather purse. "We've enough to see us through for some time, though Master Burbage told me that he'd be easier in his mind if all of us but Peter came back to London. He has places for us all, he says, and we may act with his company for our bread and meat. We can save money from our earnings and send it to Peter until—well, until the trial's over and everything's settled."

"I'll not leave Stratford while Uncle Matthew is in prison here," I told him. "And that's flat."

"Aye, nor me," growled Ben, looking fierce from under his overhanging eyebrows. "To think that long-shanked, beak-nosed skellington of a judge fined me five pound for a-buildin' of the campfire! 'Tis a unjust justice, and afore I'll sew a foot further, I'll stay and starve until Master Bailey is set free! Me an' Tom will plant ourselves right here, like unto a pair o' trees, until justice be done!"

Watkyn Bishop said dryly, "You may abide here until Doomsday, then, for I vow the old world looks to be empty of justice until then!"

Once he had finished taking care of Molly, Alan sat and told us of his long journey to London a-horseback. There was no question of a fast trip, of course, with Molly as his mount, but he declared that she bore up well, like a very Spartan, he said, and he made the eighty miles in a bit over three days.

By chance and good fortune, Alan caught Burbage just at a time when the theater master stood, as Alan put it, thigh-deep in a flood of money, and the good man had immediately given him a purse of fourteen guineas, with a smaller purse full of eating and sleeping money for him and Molly besides. Alan had returned from London with the money at hand, now able to stop at inns where good hostlers would take care of Molly. Now the poor mare looked as if she wanted nothing more than a belly full of green grass and then a week of rest.

We ate our dinner around the campfire, wooden bowls

of stew with small bits of beef and mutton floating in it like scattered islands, and then we all except Ben trooped to the jail in High Street.

Master Taylor was not on duty, but the Constable who was there finally agreed to let Peter and me back into my uncle's cell. He looked careworn and strained, and before anything he wanted to know how I did. I explained about the fever and my short hair, and then assured him, twice because he insisted, that I felt quite well again. Hesitantly, because I truly did not wish to add to his worries, I told him about the dark-clothed stranger in town who had asked about him. With a thin smile, Uncle Matthew said, "That's the least of worries, Tom. Trouble yourself no more about that."

Then he listened to what Peter had to say and nodded his agreement with Burbage's suggestion. " 'Twould be best for you all to return to London, sure," he said. He held up his hand as I began to protest. "Nay, Tom, be at ease, for I'll not insist. For one thing, Ben Fadger is a stubborn old fool, likely to land himself chin-deep in trouble, and I'd not trust him to stay here in Stratford on his own."

"Matthew," Peter said quietly, "we have enough brass now to remain a while—a week or ten days, anyway. We shall all stay until we are sure we've done everything we can for you.

From here I am going to that lawyer's house, for you will sorely need someone to advise you how to speak in court when your case comes to trial. Bailiff Hill has no objection in the world to our staying in our camp for a while—he is a good man at heart, and by my faith, I think he still wants us to act a play before we leave. Rest easy, Matthew. We will see this trouble through yet, and one day we will sit in a tavern with cups of sack in our hands and laugh about the time false charges landed you in jail."

"By your leave," Matthew said with a lopsided smile, "I think I should prefer a stoup of good honest ale. Your sack and other Spanish wines give me wind!"

It was a feeble jest, but we all laughed at it, hoping to put some heart into my poor uncle. Afterward, Peter told the others how things lay, making it sound, I thought, as though Uncle Matthew were in better spirits than he really was, and they wandered off into town. I told Peter I knew where Lawyer Collins's house was, and he and I walked to it, drawing curious stares from the good folk of Stratford.

Peter would not go to the front door of the big brick house, saying we had no standing as gentlemen to think of such a thing, so instead I led him around to the back, and Cordelia, the black-haired serving girl, let us in and then led Peter down to her master's study. I stayed in the kitchen, and when she came back, she reached up before I knew what she was about and snatched off my cap. "Oh," she said, "you have spoilt your pretty yellow hair!"

"I was sick!" I exclaimed.

"Nay, 'tis well," she said, her dark eyes merry as they drank me in. "Now you look far more manly. You are going to be a handsome husband for some lucky girl, Tom Pryne."

"And you will make a beautiful bride for some fortunate man," I told her, reaching out and hoping the flattery would make her return my cap.

But she held it teasingly beyond my reach. "Wouldst have thy cap back?" she asked coyly.

"If you please." It wasn't mine, after all, and I would need to return it to Will.

"I will sell it to you," she said, "for a kiss." She pursed her lips and leaned her pretty face forward, closing her eyes.

What was I to do? I kissed her cheek, and while she stood in momentary confusion, I took the cap from her hand. "Fie, Tom Pryne! You kiss like a schoolboy!" she accused with a laugh.

"Should I profane those cherry lips with my unworthiest touch?" I asked. That was one of Alan's speeches when I played the girl he wished to marry against her father's wishes.

"No, sweet Cordelia, you are too far above my lowly station, though I will always cherish the memory of the soft touch of thy divine cheek."

She licked her lips, and I thought I just might have gone too far. "Let me teach you how to kiss," she said in a breathy voice.

"Tom?" Peter Stonecypher was coming down the book-lined hallway, and Cordelia backed away, smiling at me.

"Come to the back door tonight after dark," she mouthed at me.

I bowed my head, thinking that I'd sooner take a stroll among hungry bears. Peter motioned me over, and in a few quick words told me how matters stood: Lawyer Collins would take ten pounds and would agree to speak with and advise my uncle, promising that he would do all he could. Still, Peter whispered with a sigh, Uncle Matthew's plight was dangerous. Without some witness, the evidence of his broken stick spoke loud against him.

"He didn't do it," I said.

"I know he didn't, lad," Peter replied firmly. "I have known Matthew Bailey man and boy these twenty years, and he never yet lost his temper even to the point of blows. Nay, Tom, you and I know that he is innocent—but the problem is to persuade a hard-headed jury that he is, and them like as not set against players, for many in Warwickshire are of a mind with the Puritans."

The Puritans despised us, I knew, for they were convinced that all plays were sinful. Not only did they attract pickpockets and low women, the Puritans argued, but the plays themselves were inspired by the Devil, the father of lies, for what is a play but one long lie? What is an actor but a hypocrite, a man who says he is one thing, a knight, a king, a beautiful lady, or what have you, but who is in reality simply a poor player strutting on a stage?

Lawyer Collins called Peter back in, and the two settled down to a long talk about people who could testify to my uncle's good character. I did not want to wait in the passage for fear of Cordelia, so I went out into the streets and slowly walked about town. I was near the stocks and the whipping-post when someone touched my shoulder, making me spin around.

It was the dark-faced man in black. He said quietly, "Is your uncle Matthew Bailey?"

"Y-yes, sir," I stammered.

"Then when next you see him, give him this message: Everything is ready." He turned and walked away without another word, leaving me to shiver at his grim appearance.

It was with low spirits that I returned to camp. The others, save only Ben, had lingered in town, now having a little money in their pockets for entertainment in the Bear or the Swan. After my illness and after all the walking I had done, I felt weak. Ben insisted that I eat more stew—"'Twill put strength in your thews and hair on your chest," he told me, though that was about the last thing I wanted. Then, very tired, I lay down to rest for an hour or two.

Toward dusk, I heard Ben muttering and stirring around again. I edged out of our tent and found that he was roasting something savory the country way, having covered the dish with the turned-over cauldron and having heaped coals on this to cook the meat. "'Tis a bit o' venison," he explained, "which Bailiff Hill sent, he hearin' that you were taken with fever, God bless him for a good man, says I. Master Stonecypher has gone to fetch the rest to supper. Here's a paper for thee, boy."

"A paper?" I asked. Ben held up a little scrap that might have been torn from the corner of a sheet. It had my name on it, and I unfolded it to read this note: "Meet me at sunset behind the church. Will. Shaxpur."

"A fellow broughted it whilst you slept," Ben said.

"A dark-faced man, wearing all black?"

"Nay, a kind of whiny, scared-looking lad, and I told him I'd see you had it from my own hand, not wanting to let him waken you up and all. Now if you'll watch the fire, I'll totter down to the river for some water."

"I'll go," I said. I crumpled the paper and tossed it onto the fire. I had no intention of meeting Will and getting in trouble all over again. "I feel better, and I need to stretch my legs."

"You sure, Tom?"

"Yes, Ben, I'm well."

"You're a good young fellow, Tom, and not like them other idle hounds. Off in town, oh, yes, a-drinkin' of ale and a-playin' of draughts or shovel-board, I'll be bound, with nary a thought for poor old Ben Fadger, a-workin' like a Christen slave among the Turks. . . ."

I picked up the wooden pail and set off down the winding path to the river. On the way, I had a nagging thought: The handwriting on the paper had not looked like Will's, but was much neater, a Chancery sort of handwriting. And that strange spelling of his name, not at all the way Will pronounced it—

Still, no one could tell a fellow how his name should be spelled, and in any case I had burned the note, so I put it out of my mind. In the dimming light I noticed then for the first time how close our camp was to Holy Trinity Church, which I saw quite plain through the trees off to the left. At the riverbank I dipped up a pail full of water, and then when I turned to lug it back to camp, I found my way blocked.

By a grinning Clarence Coste.

"Hello, imp," he said softly. "I saw you burn the paper, you little rogue."

"You let me by," I told him.

He pulled something from inside his jerkin, something pale and light, and waved it. It was a piece of the sheet I had worn while playing a ghost.

"You left something behind," he said. "I heard you when you said, 'You let me go.' 'Twas the third time I'd heard your rascally squeak, and I'm good at knowing voices. I had to think and think to place yours, but finally I brought to mind the boy who roamed with the players, the rogue I saw in the churchyard with that wicked Will."

"You'd better let me pass," I warned. "My friends are just up the hillside behind you."

"And who's that behind *you?*" he asked with an evil leer and a nod over my shoulder.

I should have known better—as a trick it was miserable, not a patch on Will's elaborate plans—but there had been two of them back at the bridge, and I could not help whipping around to see if Giles Speight truly stood behind me.

He was not, but in an instant Clarence Coste sprang forward, seized me, and struck me a hard blow on the side of my head. All the world exploded in yellow light, and then I fell into darkness and fainted quite away.

Eighteen

"... interred with their bones ..."

I came to my senses in utter darkness, with the dry scent of dust and the reek of decay strong in my nose. I lay on my side on a rough stone surface, and when I moved, my head pounded in protest. I explored my head with my hand, feeling the strange short-cut hair and beneath it, a lump the size of a partridge egg. My stomach lurched with sickness, and I turned to one side and coughed up some foul-tasting vomit. It did not perfume the fetid air, either, but made the stench worse.

I rolled away from it and pushed myself first to my knees, and then rose slowly, afraid that my head would thump into something. The air was so stale that I found my chest heaving and gasping for breath. Where was I? I groped forward and touched something smooth and round, like a ball. My fingers felt a flare of the hard material, then an empty hole. Two of them.

I was feeling a human skull, and next to it I found another and another and another.

"Charnel house!" I groaned, knowing then where Coste had thrown me. I was in the bone-house next to the church, surrounded by skeletons long since taken up from the churchyard, dismembered and arrayed on shelves and in piles. I knew well how these things were done. In London I had seen whole vaults piled ceiling-high with staring skulls.

It is a funny thing, but though I should have been terrified at that moment of spirits and ghosts, I felt nothing but anger at Coste and at myself—he for clouting me so hard and taking me so easily, and myself for being such a dunce-fool as to let myself be caught. Perhaps his fist had knocked a bit of sense into my aching head, but I saw with clarity that the note from "Will" had been his work. He had tried to lure me to the church, at sunset! Perhaps he was the one who had given the scrap of paper to Ben Fadger in the first place, for to Ben any male much under the age of sixty qualified as a "lad."

"Stupid," I told myself. "Stupid, stupid!" I tried to remember how the charnel house looked from the outside, to get some notion of where the door might be. With one hand on the shelves of skulls, I inched around, groping in the dark with the other hand. I felt first a stone wall, came to a stone step and climbed it, then another three of them. At the top I stood on a narrow sort of platform, and with my hands I felt first a wooden jamb, and then the door itself. It was barred from the outside, of course. I pounded on it and shouted, but no response came. How long had I been in that faint? It might be deep night by this time. Surely the players would have missed me. By now old Ben must have toddled down the path to see what had become of his pail of water.

All my beating at the door and yelling did was to make my head ache yet more dismally, so I stopped and felt again until I found the door handle. It had a great keyhole in the plate, and I knelt to put my eye to it. Either it had been stopped up or else it was dark as midnight outside. I put my nose beside the keyhole and snuffed in some cool, fresh air. What could I do? What could I use to break out of this horrible place? Bones? I doubted they would serve, being so breakable themselves. But what if the sexton stored his spades and picks in here?

I flailed through the darkness but found nothing, no tool or device that might help me. It seemed I was interred with these bones until Master Coste took it into his warped brain to let me out.

With that realization, fear came at last. I started to

shudder, unable to control my feelings. Locked in the dark with hundreds of the dead! I began to imagine the most wretched things, cold hands about to grip me by the throat, fiends smoking with the flames of Hades lurking in corners to snatch my soul from my body, even the hound of hell that we had come roaring out of a trapdoor in our *Murder Aveng'd*. In my terrified mind I thought such a beast of Satan might be lying in wait, tired of chewing on an old dry bone and hungry for warm and living flesh.

Then I thought of my uncle's once telling Michael Moresby how to overcome stage fright: "Clear thy mind of all but the task before thee, lad. Set your attention on that, as a sailor watches a steadfast star, and leave no room for fears or doubt!"

"I will get out," I told myself, clenching my hands into fists. "I will get out somehow, and I'll be revenged on that mad sexton Clarence Coste! I will get out. . . ."

Did it help? Maybe. At any rate, I managed to quell the knocking of my knees and the chattering of my teeth. I thought that the skulls I had first felt rested on what seemed to be heavy wooden shelves. If I could pull down one of the shelves, perhaps I could use it or a plank from it as a battering-ram, I thought. We had pounded down many a castle door onstage when we played the wicked French in *The Siege of Gaillard*.

I soon persuaded myself that such a hope was vain, for the shelves had been firmly bolted to the stone walls, and I could not budge one, no, not an inch. "Oh!" I shouted in fury. From a pile I grabbed a long bone, probably a leg bone, and carried that back to the steps and the door. I beat on the door with this, producing a drumming that I thought should arouse every soul in Stratford, but nothing happened, save the noise made my headache worse.

I threw the bone away, furious with myself for not being bright enough to find a way out. Then I heard what might have been going on for minutes: Someone outside was tapping on the door! I felt for the door handle and keyhole and stooped to call out, "Help! I'm locked in!"

"I know! I don't have the key!"

I groaned. Will Shakespeare. Just my luck on this luckless night.

"Get help!"

"Nay, he may come back to kill you! I'll find something to break the lock. Wait, for I've already unbarred the door—if we can just get the lock open, I'll have you out in the wink of an eye!"

I felt the far side of the door jamb again, then went back to the keyhole. "Will! Will, listen to me! I think I know a way! Will?"

He had gone, the maddening boy. I stamped my feet out of the mere need to be doing *something* until I heard some ringing clangs. "Wait! Wait! What are you doing?"

"I found a spade!" Will called back. "I'm trying to break the lock!"

"You'll never do it with a spade! Will, are the door hinges outside?"

A moment of silence, and then he said, "Yes! Maybe I can work out the pins!"

Then such a scraping and rattling came, sounding as though Will were trying to plane the door smooth with that dull spade. That fell quiet, though, and a moment later I heard a clink. "Will! D'you hear me?"

"Aye! One's out!"

"Listen! Pick up that hinge-pin and use it to drive out the others! Put it in the bottom of the hinge and strike it upward!"

"Yes! Well thought!" I could faintly hear Will grunting, then muffled pounding, and finally the tinkle as a second hinge pin fell out. Almost there!

More taps, but then Will called, "The top one is too rusty! It won't budge! I've a thought, though. Stand back from the door, for I'm going to push!"

The door did not open, for one hinge pin, the topmost,

still held. Will grunted, and I heard the splintering of dry old wood. The top hinge plate was pulling loose! On just part of the hinge and on the lock-bolt, the wooden door pivoted inward, letting in a blessed breath of fresh air. "Can you squeeze beneath?" Will asked anxiously.

"Not with it tilted toward me! Let me push it outward, toward you! You grab the edge and lift!"

I sat and braced my feet against the door, shoved the left edge forward, and with more cracks of splintering wood it tilted out into the night. Flat on my belly, I wormed my way through the small triangular opening, scraping my back but eager to be free of that dark house of death. I sprang up, my head reeling, and hugged Will. "For this rescue, much thanks! Why, you're shaking—you're like ice!"

"Not from cold. I've always feared this place," confessed Will with a gasp. "When I was only ten, Costard caught me playing in the churchyard and hauled me over, showing me the dead men's bones and threatening to lock me up until I was naught but bone myself! Ugh, it makes me sick to think on't. Let's go, quickly."

I felt much moved that Will had faced his fears and outbraved them to come to help me, but this seemed no time for long speeches. "How came you here?" I asked as we hurried among the gravestones.

"Someone left a note for me, telling me you needed me to meet you here—"

"Coste," I told him. "He gave me another such note. He must be about somewhere. We have to get away, fast. Let's find the constable. I think what Coste did to me must have broken some law."

"Back to town, then," Will said. Dim moonlight glimmered, and in its deceptive, weak illumination, we threaded our way among the crazily tilting old headstones, until we were almost out into the lane and away.

And then something reared up in front of us, gurgling, groaning, and coughing: a black shadowy thing that made me shriek in fear.

"Now I have you," gurgled the hoarse voice of Clarence Coste, and the shape fell forward and crashed to earth.

Nineteen

"That skull had a tongue in it,
and could sing once . . ."

Will drew back, and I realized he wielded the spade as if it were a club and was about to hit the fallen Coste, who lay twitching on the ground, groaning.

"No!" I called, just in time. Will broke his swing, and in the darkness the spade whished wide, chopping harmlessly into the earth. "I think he's hurt!" I said.

"Good!" panted Will.

I reached down and shook the fallen man. "Master Coste! Master Coste! What's amiss with you?"

"I bleed," he groaned.

"Who's there!" It was a familiar voice, the voice of the vicar of Stratford, Mr. Smart. He carried a lantern, and in its yellow glare he weaved his way through the headstones. "What ungodly din is this, for shame?"

"Help!" I called. "'Tis your sexton, Coste!"

"Sexton? Grave digger!" said Vicar Smart. "Drunk again, I make no doubt?"

"He's hurt," I said. The minister drew near and held his lantern high. Coste had rolled onto his back and lay breathing hard, puffing his cheeks out and in. He wore his dirty brown breeches and jerkin, but the right side of the jerkin was all dark and shiny with blood.

Smart knelt and said, "How is it with you, Coste?"

Coste's eyes fluttered open and rolled. He coughed a spray of blood. Then he chuckled grimly. "I bleed, sir, but am not killed! Fetch me a surgeon, in the name of God!"

"One of you boys—" began Smart, but before he could finish, Will was away, throwing back the words "I'll seek out Dr. Wells!" over his shoulder.

"Who did this to you, Coste?" asked the preacher.

"He that had the most to gain and the most to lose," Coste murmured. "Lord, it hurts!"

"Lie still. I'll stanch the blood if I can." The parson, a small man, tore a strip from his shirt, folded it, and opened Coste's jerkin. He reached inside with his pad of cloth and pressed it tight. "Lie still until the doctor comes."

Coste's rolling eyes had stopped when he saw me. He grinned with bloody teeth and muttered,

"Left alone in a house of bone,
    And 'scaped to a world of blood!"

"Sirrah, be still!" the vicar said. He looked up at me and said, "He's drunk again. He's been often so these last days—I don't know where the rogue finds the money."

"I give you a riddle," Coste said, ignoring the preacher and seemingly speaking only to me. His face clenched with pain, and in a weak voice he chanted,

"The eyes of the dead watch where we tread,
    They follow us from on high;
In dark do they dwell and they can tell
    A tale to make brothers sigh!
Many a foul deed of wrath and greed
    May be found in a dead man's head!"

"What foolishness is this?" asked Vicar Smart. "Be still, sir, if you want to live!"

Time seemed to drag, but not many minutes passed before Will and the doctor came hurrying along, the doctor holding a lantern of his own. "I found him at home!" Will said. "Just past the college!"

"Who have we here?" Dr. Wells asked, kneeling. "Costard! Well, my man, you've lost more blood than you can well spare. Who did this mischief to you, sir?"

"Nobody," Coste said defiantly, shivering but trying to muster what sounded like a scornful laugh. "I myself."

"I would not lie if my soul were as lightly tied to earth as yours," the doctor observed.

" 'Tis but a scratch. You'll stitch it up again," Coste said in a low, weak voice. "I would not ha' killed the lads, mind. Just locked 'em in until I got my gold and left this town."

The doctor cut away the jerkin and bent to examine the wound. I heard him take in a sharp breath, as though what he saw disturbed him. "Don't jest, Coste, but tell me in sober earnest, who stabbed you thus?"

"The devil," said Coste, his voice hardly more than a whisper. "Patch me up, patch me up, and I'll do well enough." He coughed hard, fetched three great gasping breaths, and the last rattled in his throat. His heels drummed the earth, and then his joints went loose and he sprawled with no more life than a doll sewn of patches.

"He is gone," the doctor said. "A fool to the last. He was

drunk. He drinks at the Bear. Maybe someone there knows who did this to him."

"He said he stabbed himself," the vicar said.

"And he lied, sir. Well, well, this will be a nine days' wonder! No man-killing in Stratford in ages, and now two within ten days!"

"Sirs," I said, "Coste struck me on the head early this evening, and then he locked me in the bone-house."

"What?" roared the doctor. "Why, you didn't stab him yourself, did you, lad?"

"No, sir!"

"I wouldn't have blamed you if you had. Will Shakespeare, he tried that caper on you once, did he not? Your father told me of it."

Will shivered. "Yes, sir. A few years back. He said he'd lock me alone in a house of bone—"

"He said the same rhyme to me, before he died," I said.

"'Tis true," the preacher told him. "That and some other foolish rhyme that I cannot remember—dead men's heads and what not."

"Oh, sir," said Will urgently. "Saving your grace, try to recall Costard's rhyme!"

"Nay, I cannot. 'Twas nothing but his usual foolishness. I cannot call the words to mind."

"I can," I said, and recited Coste's odd words:

> "The eyes of the dead watch where we tread,
> They follow us from on high;
> In dark do they dwell and they can tell
> A tale to make brothers sigh!
> Many a foul deed of wrath and greed
> May be found in a dead man's head!"

"Yes!" Will exclaimed. "Now I know!"

"Know what?" asked the doctor.

"I know who killed Edmund Speight," said Will. "And then who killed Clarence Coste!"

The two men straightened, and the minister raised his lantern high. Will stood pale-faced but sturdy as a statue, back straight and staring defiance at us all. In that instant I finally understood why Will falsely thought I was smaller than he. Will Shakespeare stood on the shoulders of his own imagination, and in his mind that made him a Colossus!

Both doctor and minister began to ask the same question at once: "What do you—" And both broke off at the same instant.

Will, in as cold and determined a voice as ever I heard

stage hero use, said, "Send for the two Speight sons, and I will show you!"

Not just the two Speight sons, but half of Stratford had joined us in the vestry of the church some hour later. John Shakespeare looked vexed, but Will insisted that he knew what he was doing, and Richard Hill and a justice of the peace told Master Shakespeare to wait to chastise his son until there was more reason.

When all had gathered, with Giles and Francis Speight seated as far apart as they could get in that space, Will said, "Now, to begin with, I believe that Master Edmund Speight was killed by being struck with the stick that belonged to Tom's uncle, Matthew Bailey—but Master Bailey did not strike him." He explained that my uncle had told us how he came out of the Swan before Speight left, how he needed to answer a call of nature, and how he had leaned the walking-stick against the wall near the inn door.

Will continued, "And we know from Cordelia Blackstone, serving-girl to Lawyer Collins, that Speight did not have his own walking-stick with him that day. She said he called at the lawyer's house before sunset, and that he limped so badly she had to help him back into the saddle." He turned and asked, "Francis, where is your father's walking-stick?"

"It is at home, in the chimney-corner where he always kept it," said Francis.

"Because he'd thought to ride to the lawyer's house and ride straight back home," Will explained. "He did not believe he'd have need of a stick. But by the time he got my father and the doctor to sign his document, his leg no doubt ached from his tramping through town seeking witnesses. So as he stepped out, he saw a stick leaning against the wall—and he took it."

"My father was no thief!" said Giles Speight.

"It was there," Will said firmly, "and his leg hurt, and he took it. He mounted his horse, the great bay gelding, and rode toward the bridge. Who fetched Francis to the place where his father was killed?"

"I did," said one of the watchmen. "I rode out to the farm and he rode back with me."

"On the bay?"

"No, on the gray mare."

"Francis, was the bay gelding in the stable?"

"Aye," said Francis. "I found him outside the house past dark, and thinking that Father had come in too tired to take care of him, I took off his saddle and tack, rubbed him down, and put him in the stall. I had hardly finished that when Master Stafford there came for me with the news. I saddled Dapple, and rode in with him as he told you."

"Then it is plain," Will said. "Edmund was riding the gelding across the bridge when he met someone. The two of them had words; I think Edmund was in such a temper that he swung his stolen walking-stick at the person he met. That man seized the stick and pulled him off the horse. The horse bolted for home, as horses will. And when the old man rose up threatening and maybe fighting, the other man struck him a crushing blow with the stick, so hard that the stick itself broke in two. Then I think the murderer threw his part of the broken stick into the Avon and fled away."

"How did the head of the stick get to the players' camp?" asked Constable Taylor, frowning.

"Someone took it to where Ben Fadger found it. The same man who rolled Edmund Speight's body over the parapet of the bridge. The same one who then took money from the murderer, because he had been lurking in the darkness and had seen the murder done. Clarence Coste, who now is dead himself."

"Stabbed," the doctor confirmed.

"Stabbed by the man whose money he was demanding as the price of silence," Will said. "We know he had more money than he'd ever had before—he's been drinking it away!"

"You cannot prove any of this," the lawyer, Mr. Collins said.

"Yes, I can," Will insisted. "Because Costard not only took away the broken head of the staff, leaving it on the pathway so someone would find it and think the murderer had fled to the south of town—"

"Why would he have done that?" asked the minister.

"Because he planned to bleed money from the real killer," Will said. "He didn't want that man arrested and put beyond his reach. I say, Costard took not only the broken stick, but also some folded papers from the old man. His last will."

"Can you prove this?" the lawyer asked, still sounding as if he doubted it.

"Coste told Tom here where he hid the papers, so yes, I can," Will responded. He turned to me. "Tell them the rhyme Coste said to you before he died."

Feeling worse stage fright than I had ever known in all my life, I recited the words that the preacher had called nonsense.

"There," Will said when I finished. "A foul deed can be found in a dead man's head. And a deed is a legal document, just as a will is. Coste hid the will in the charnel house."

The minister had a key, but we hardly needed it. When the bone-house door was unlocked, its one remaining hinge gave way and the whole thing fell inward with a crash of lumber. In the wavering yellow light of the lanterns, the skulls on their shelves seemed to leer down and glare at us. "It will be up high," Will said in a shaky voice.

And up high, on the highest shelves of skulls, they found it some little time after. It had been rolled up and thrust in through the eye socket of an ancient skull and had lodged in the brain pan, but Constable Taylor shook it out.

"There," Will said. "Edmund Speight's last will." He turned and said, "And you will find that it leaves everything to one of the two Speight brothers. The one left out is the one who killed his own father. And that one has to be—Giles Speight!"

Lawyer Collins, who had seized and unfolded the rectangle of paper and who bent over it, reading in the light of the preacher's lantern, looked up.

"You are quite wrong," he said.

⤟ Twenty ⤠

"Accursed fatal hand,
That hath contriv'd this woeful tragedy!"

Over the crowd's gabble, the lawyer raised his voice: "There is a long preamble here in old Edmund's hand. He rants about the expense he has been to over the years, changing his will so many times—though I protest, my fees are quite low, extraordinarily reasonable—at any rate, Edmund says here, 'If I leave my lands and money to one, the other then turns on me, and so I shall leave nothing to neither of them.' Young Master Shakespeare is very clever to have found this will, but it does not cut one of the sons off. It cuts them both off!"

Without going into the legal whys and wherefores, Mr. Collins told us all that Speight's last, spiteful will disinherited Giles and Francis alike, the former for a lazy wastrel, the latter for a disobedient wretch. Instead, the whole estate, land, house, and fortune, was to pass to a cousin of Edmund's, a Mr. Foynt of Snitterfield, a very elderly, feeble man.

Will looked crushed. "But—it had to be—"

"It did not," said Giles angrily. "Had you asked, you would have found that from six that evening until nearly midnight I was in the company of half a dozen men, playing at cards. They can all testify to that!"

A sad voice said, "Will was almost right, though."

Everyone looked at Francis Speight. With a sorrowful shake of his head he said, "I did not mean to kill my father."

"Francis, no—" Will said.

"Yes," Francis said firmly. "And the thought that an honest man is imprisoned for my offense has gnawed at me this past week. 'Tis a rank and stinking offense that must make the angels stop their noses! Before God, though, my masters, I did not intend it. When I learned at the farm that my father had gone into town, I feared he might be doing just what he had threatened. I rode in and met him on the bridge. It happened almost as Will Shakespeare there said— we had words, he swung a stick at me, and I caught it. The horses reared and we both fell off. When we stood, I held the stick. My father called me—names that I would take from no man. In blind anger at him I struck, struck harder than I meant, and he dropped down stone dead. The stick had broken short. His own horse had run off; I threw the broken end of the stick into the river, leaped into my saddle, and returned home. I just had time to put both horses away before the watchman came to collect me."

"And Costard?" the constable asked.

"Came to me the next day and told me he had seen it all. Yes, he had put my father's body into the river. Coste wanted money from me. I gave it to him. He asked me to meet him in the shadows behind the church tonight, and there he wanted more. He told me he had cleverly rewritten the new will, forging my father's handwriting, to leave everything to me, and if I paid him, he would tell me where to find it. He wanted the money first. A thousand pounds, as though my father had really kept that much gold about! I told Coste I did not have it. He said that I would never find the will, then, and threatened to tell everyone what he had seen. He cursed me. I struck him, he drew his dagger and slashed at me, we fought—and somehow in our fighting we fell and the dagger pierced his side. I wrested the dagger from his bloody grip and threw it into the river and ran away. I did not know he had a deadly hurt, I swear I did not, and Will, I did not know he meant you and your friend when he babbled of having someone locked up."

"Why did you not tell us all this earlier?" asked the lawyer heavily.

"Because I am in love," Francis said simply. "Because I had hoped to marry. But now, with no land, no money, and no hopes, what have I left to lose?"

Constable Taylor coughed. "I must take you into custody," he said.

What an uproar then fell about us! Before the night was over, we found how close Will had come to the truth—for while Francis confessed he had given Coste money to keep him quiet about the death of old Edmund, so Giles bitterly admitted he had been paying him to keep the will secret, for Coste had lied and had told him that the new will was in favor of his brother, showing him one page that seemed to point that way. When Giles said that, Will spoke up suddenly, asking a question that put puzzled looks on all faces: "You came that night to see my ghost, but why did Coste come with you?"

"Because the letter read like the work of someone mad, and I thought it must truly have come from Costard," Giles said. "I sought him out and asked him, and he claimed it was none of his sending, but he would go with me to learn what villain was trying to steal his money—*his* money!"

The final word fell to the massive Lawyer Collins, who

heaved a deep sigh. "Poor foolish old Edmund Speight! My masters, 'tis plain to me, for I knew him right well, that this last will of his, this holograph instrument as we term it in law, was meant to put contrition into the hearts of both his sons and make them obey him, for I am sure that within a day or two he would have boasted to them both that he had disinherited them entirely. Then Edmund would have waited to see which of them would come crawling to him in penitent humility. Oh, I knew him down to the very bone, I tell you, and I will lay you any odds that had he found time to cool his hot temper before that fatal meeting on the bridge, had he lived but another two weeks, or even one week, he would have made up with either Francis or Giles or both before the new moon turned old again. Then we would have had yet another will, and beyond that no doubt another and another. The peevish old fellow did not expect to die. My friends, in the midst of life we be in death, and no man knows when his last hour might come."

There was nothing to add but the parson's "amen," and when the gathering broke up, I was glad enough to walk back to camp and seize what sleep I could.

Early in the morning the constable set my uncle free. The judge released Ben Fadger from his bond, which made him grumble that the court should have paid him interest on such a sizable loan.

Will asked me to breakfast, and so I was in his house when John Shakespeare came in, his face ashen. "Such news," he said. "Giles Speight left town this morning, swearing never to return. And I've heard that Julia Cabot has drowned herself!" His voice broke with the pity of it. "A Shottery man told me. She threw herself into the river and drowned. And Francis Speight is dead."

"No!" shouted Will.

John Shakespeare nodded sadly. "They told him of Julia's doing away with herself. He asked to be left alone, and the fools did it. An hour later they found he had torn his shirt to ribbons, braided them into a kind of rope, and had hanged himself in his cell. Such senseless death, such a horrible—"

Will ran out. I followed him to the back garden, where I heard him sobbing bitterly. He had hunched beneath a young tree there, and he sat in a ball of misery. "You couldn't help it, Will," I told him.

"My friend is dead," he said bitterly. "And his sweetheart, that pretty girl, has drowned herself because of what I did! Oh, Viola, everything I've done has brought woe to those I liked best!"

"But you set my uncle free of false charges," I pointed out. "And you resolved the question of two murders, when no grown man could have done it."

Will rocked back and forth. "Viola, I only wanted a bit of excitement in this dull town. I didn't want—this tragedy."

"Perhaps it was your fate," I said soothingly. "Some divinity shapes these things, though we cannot always see God's hand at work."

"We don't believe in predestination," Will muttered. "Not Catholics."

I stood over him, wanting to offer him comfort, to tell him that he had done more good than perhaps he knew. I had told him once that I hated all Catholics—but now I almost wished that his parents had been mine, so kind and caring they were. Perhaps I had begun to understand the world of difference between simple Christian charity and the twisted, hateful shape into which evil men had warped it. Though I tried to think of a way, I could not quite put that into words that Will might understand.

I am only a player, not a writer of plays. I could not find the right words to say all these things. And so I did the only thing I could do to ease his grief: I merely sat beside him, in the scant shade of a young tree, and put my arm around his shoulders, held him close, and let him weep and weep and weep.

∞ Twenty-one ∞

"... such stuff as dreams are made on ..."

In the next few days, everyone in Stratford buzzed with the news of what had happened, and of the strange surprising turn of events that had freed my uncle. They all wanted to buy our men drinks and hear them speak of the case, and they all clamored to hear us act.

My uncle declared 'twould be a plain sin to give up such a chance, and so we stayed the weekend and gave our plays the next week. Bailiff Hill, mindful I think of all the trouble my uncle had been to, generously put twenty shillings in our purse after the Mayor's Show (how I hated that angel's wig!); and then for two days following so many curious people crowded and crammed into the market to see us act our other plays that, ere our play-acting was all over, we had grown richer by full forty-two shillings and sixpence more, a golden reward indeed.

Yet through those days Will remained gloomy and downcast. My uncle had come to know Will, and on Wednesday afternoon he asked me to take him to the Shakespeare house. First he spoke with John and Mary Shakespeare, and then, back out in the garden again, he spoke to Will. "Lad," he said, "I do thank you for what you did to free me. Now I have to ask for another favor, to my great shame."

"What is that?" asked Will.

My uncle made a face. "We have this play—'tis called the *Comedy of Lovers*—that I dearly want to act, but there's a part in it we can't fill: a quarreling old grandfather. Ben Fadger has done it before, but he's taken against your town and flat refuses. Tom tells me you are quick of wit and have a good memory."

Will gave me a faint smile, his eyes still red from weeping. "Aye," he said. "I do."

"Then do you think you could memorize the part and perform it with us? It is not long, just some eighteen or twenty lines, but it is a great source of laughter."

Will looked down at the ground, and for a second I thought he would turn my uncle down. Then, with a smile, he whispered, "I think I could do it."

I rehearsed the lines with him, and he soon had them by heart. Relieved at not having to play the part, Ben fitted Will out finely in a long white beard and wig, and in the market square Will sat in a chair, crabbed-up and bent over, and he piped his voice in a comic treble note as he misheard everything that was said to him:

Dickon: Grandfather, would you have some cheese and bread?

Grandfather: Nay, my grandson, my knees are well and I am not dead!

And in the latter part of the play:

Romeus: Old man, I want thy grand-daughter to wed as bride!

Grandfather: Young man, I made no grand water, nor am I wet with pride!

Silly stuff, but the people of Stratford knew their rascally Will and liked well the droll way that he said the lines, so they all howled with laughter. As the young girl, Emilye, I toyed with Alan as my would-be lover, Romeus, and petted my little dog—yes, we even found a place in the show for

Hamnet's dog, Crab, and out in the front row of the audience the black-haired boy puffed up visibly with pride.

After that final show, I slipped into the Shakespeare house with Will, and we hurried upstairs to his parents' bedroom, where his mother had an apron hanging on a peg. I clinked five shillings into the pocket, knowing that she would know whence it came, and hoping she would know how grateful I felt for everything she had done in her kindness of heart.

"I hate to see you go, Viola," Will told me sorrowfully. "After all the ills I caused, I'll have not a friend in Stratford. Poor Francis! And poor Julia! Everyone will hate me."

My uncle met us out front—he had been talking to Will's father—and he heard something of what Will said. "Walk with us," he told the boy. Once we were well away from the crowded streets, Uncle Matthew turned and said softly, "Master Will, you are yet young in the world. Trust me, you will find time enough in your life to weep and grieve, yes, but also time to laugh and rejoice. That is a man's lot in life, lad, so take the foul and the fair all with a full and ready heart, as a man must. You have a good head on your shoulders and good talents in your soul. Make the most of them, Will."

He lowered his voice and said, "And be happy for this:

Your father has just now given me word he received from a priest passing secretly through town that Viola's parents are well and safely away in Ireland."

Will slumped. "A priest!" he said. "The stranger in town, a dark-faced man, dressed all in black! A priest, of course he was!"

"Oh!" I cried out, and clapped my hand over my mouth to keep from shouting in joy. "I was to tell you he said, 'Everything is ready.' I forgot!"

My uncle patted my shoulder. "No matter, for John Shakespeare had a much fuller message for me, and now it remains for us to act on it. I'll shape our course so we pass through Bristol ere turning toward London," he said, his voice rough with emotion. "In Bristol we'll find a ship, and while the others go back to Master Burbage, you and I will sail to Ireland. I'll not return to England until I see you well bestowed with my sister and her husband, and there you will be safe at last."

"God be thanked," I said, fighting back joyful tears. "And Will, thank your father for me, for this is the best news I've heard in a year!"

"Say your farewells, then, you two—but be quick about it." Uncle Matthew went on to where our men already waited with the loaded wagon.

"Won't I ever see you again?" Will asked, staring at the ground.

"I am sure you will," I lied, for who knew what paths lay before me? "Now listen to me, Will Shakespeare: Far from here, away in London, Master Burbage has built a wonderful thing, a theater so that we poor actors will have a home and hearth and not be forced to go about in this wild and wandering way! When you are older, Will, you must make your way to London."

"I can't—"

"You can do what you set your mind to!" I said, fighting back a sob. "Find Mr. Burbage there! Tell him you acted with us! Until then, learn to sing, and dance, and play the lute, and how to wield a sword! Make yourself ready to be a real player."

"D-do you think I could?"

"I think you can do anything you want, Will! I've never known a boy like you. Mayhap you'll even find me in London, too, where I'll no longer be a player, but certainly I'll always be one who loves the theater. And in London, Will, and in the theater you can do such wonderful things! You can tread upon a stage, and act, and write plays of your own, and bring out of your fancy men and women who will live for their hour and move an audience to tears or to laughter! You have to do it, Will. Stratford is too small for you. Promise me you will."

"I—we'll see. I . . . I—oh, Viola!" For one time in his life, Will Shakespeare stood dumbstruck. I kissed him quickly on the cheek, then hurried away to the wagon, where Alan helped me up and where Ben Fadger was already sewing and cursing, just as if our whole time in Stratford had blown away like so much smoke and fog, leaving nothing behind.

"A fine day for traveling," my uncle said, shaking the reins. Molly and Dunce ambled forward, and the wagon rumbled off on the road.

I turned back and waved. Will stood on the empty ground where we had camped and waved back, for as long as I could see him. And then the road curved, and he faded from my view.

Knowing he would never fade from my memory, I turned around in the wagon and for the first time in months looked ahead with hope to whatever the future might bring.

Finis

Here's a preview of the next exciting historical mystery
by Bailey MacDonald:

THE
SECRET
OF THE
SEALED ROOM

✺ One ✺

WHAT SIGNIFIES YOUR PATIENCE, IF YOU CAN'T FIND IT
WHEN YOU WANT IT?
—POOR RICHARD'S ALMANAC

My name is Patience, but I have little of that with all those
in Boston who keep telling me what a bad girl I am. When
I learned my letters, the very first sentence I could read
proved a harsh and scolding one: *In Adam's fall, we sinned all.*
In church of a Sunday when the parson preaches about the
sins and failings of women, I would swear he gazes straight
at me with a stern, disapproving look. And of course Mrs.
Worth, to whom my father bound me as a servant when
my mother died, always assured me that I am a lazy, sullen,
disobedient, and wicked wretch, destined to come to an
evil end.

But let me begin at the beginning, on a September day in
the year of our Lord 1721. Mrs. Worth had rung her bell for

me early, before the sun had risen, and I found her groaning in her bed. "Child," she said, "run and fetch Moll Bacon, and hurry!"

"I must dress—," I began, only to be cut short by her angry words: "Go, I tell you! Go, and hurry!"

Still I dressed hastily, then set out running from the Worth house, on its low hill overlooking the Roxbury Road, right down Orange Street and so to Newbury Street and then into the still-sleeping heart of Boston. Mists crept through the streets like silent cats, gray in the dimness before dawn. Hardly any faint yellow lights showed, but I knew the way right well: along Marlborough and Cornhill streets south of the Common, then a sharp turn onto Water Street, with its narrow shops and dark, looming warehouses. A lonely rooster crowed somewhere, and then another answered him, and another. Dogs barked as I hurried through the damp and the dark, feeling the wet cobbles slippery beneath the thin soles of my worn-out shoes, shivering in the coolness of the early-September morning.

The fishermen were up already, of course. Far ahead, down toward the Long Wharf, I could see the reddish glows of their lanterns on the face of the night. I even heard a distant fisherman's gruff, growling voice singing the words of a doleful old ballad:

"As I walked forth one summer's day
To view the meadows green and gay,
A pleasant bower I espied
Standing fast by the riverside,
And in't a maiden I heard cry:
Alas! Alas! There's none e'er loved as I."

Having no time to listen, I hurried on until I came to a great warehouse that smelled strongly of fish, and I began to count the buildings beyond it, two, three, four, and there I turned into the pitch-dark, narrow alley that leads back around the corner to Moll Bacon's cottage. Though small, it nestles in a neat and clean yard blooming with little herb and flower gardens, and the white paint on the house and its picket fence is smart and fresh-looking, or at least it is in sunlight. In the darkness both seemed to glow a pearly gray.

Early though it was, as I approached Moll Bacon's cottage, I glimpsed candlelight through a window, and when I rapped at the door, the old midwife opened it at once. She was already dressed, as if she really had the second sight that some in Boston whispered fearfully about. "What is it, girl?" she asked gruffly.

I did not flinch from her, though she had a dark face sharp as an Indian tomahawk, all sharp angles and cutting edges, and beneath her heavy black brows her scowl made her look as fierce as the old Abenaki warrior she claimed as her grandfather. "My mistress wants you," I said.

She grunted and tilted her head. "You are the Martin girl. You belong to Abedela Worth."

"I belong to myself," I said with as much spirit as I could, meeting her dark-eyed gaze. "But I work for Mrs. Worth."

She laughed then, one sharp, gruff bark, and she turned half away from me as she reached for something—a large basket, I saw. "Come, then, Patience Martin, and let's see to the woman you work for."

Moll did not lock the door, and answering my glance rather than my words she said, "None in Boston would dare come in without my permission. Fast walking will warm us, girl. Carry this."

I took the basket, which was covered with a calico cloth and as heavy as a load of stone, but no answer did I make. Only a month or so earlier, when Mrs. Worth first suspected that she was with child, had I met this strange woman. That very first time she had curtly told me not to call her Mistress Bacon, or even Goody Bacon, as some of the older people did. "Moll's my name, and that's what you shall call me," she had said. Since that first time, Moll Bacon had come to the house often, sometimes two or three times each week, for

Mrs. Worth was having a hard time of it. I should have felt sorry for her, a poor widow woman whose husband was three months drowned and herself four months gone in pregnancy. I could not feel much sympathy for her, though, with my own father dead in the same ship as her husband, and my future so clouded, and her hand so hard and so ready to slap me for any small failing on my part. Perhaps my lack of compassion was another measure of my badness.

We trotted along side by side in the slowly growing light of dawn. Moll spoke little, but once she suddenly asked, for no reason that I could see, "How old are you, girl?"

"Fourteen last month," I replied, panting. I understood that Moll Bacon herself was no more than forty-five, though I thought she looked a good twenty years older, and she made a good pace of it, so that I had to scurry to keep up, never getting a chance to catch my breath. We reached the house, and I saw lights in the downstairs windows. The chickens were awake now, murmuring and scratching about the backyard. I started toward them, for Mrs. Worth was very strict about my never coming in through the front door, but that opened as Moll and I stepped into the yard. A tall, thin, gray man beckoned impatiently for us to come in that way: Mr. Richard Worth, Mrs. Worth's brother-in-law. He was past fifty—Mrs. Worth's husband, Jared, his older brother, had been sixty when he drowned—and he had a sharp, waspish manner. He and his son, David, were Mrs. Worth's nearest neighbors. "She's very ill," snapped Mr. Richard. "You'd best hurry." He turned his gaze on me. "Don't stand there with your basket! Go with her. Make yourself useful!"

I gave him a barely polite nod of my head, and together with Moll I hurried up the stair to the second-floor bedroom, where my mistress lay moaning dolefully.

Mrs. Worth, her already thin cheeks sunken, lay back on her feather pillow, her brown hair hidden beneath her nightcap. Her red-rimmed eyes glittered in anger as we came into the gloomy room. "Why did you take so long?" she demanded in an unnaturally hoarse voice.

"I came as quickly as I could," replied Moll. "Are you in pain?"

"My head is splitting, and my stomach is cramping terribly. I am afraid I might lose the baby."

Moll took the basket from me, then pointed to the fine beeswax candle that Mrs. Worth used to read by at night. "Child, light that for me."

"No," grumbled Mrs. Worth. "It's too expensive to burn idly while there is daylight. Open the curtains instead."

"Yes, ma'am," I said. It did not do to cross her in anything, however small. I drew and tied back the curtains from the room's two windows, and the milky light of early day spilled into the dim bedroom. I could not help thinking that the candle would have given Moll considerably more illumination.

"I need you to take this," Moll said, handing me a small, nearly weightless cloth bag that felt as if it contained dried herbs, "and boil it in a pint of water. When the pot begins to bubble, drop this in, and boil it until you can count to a hundred, slowly—you can count, can't you?"

"Of course I can count!"

"She is a tetchy, forward child," said Mrs. Worth, adding a dismal groan.

Moll ignored her: "Count to a hundred, slowly, and then take the pot off the stove and allow it to steep for a quarter of an hour. Then pour off the tea that is brewed, put it in a mug, and bring it to me. Throw away the bag, for the medicine will have no virtue for a second boiling."

"I understand."

Downstairs Mr. Richard was standing beside a fire he had just lit in the parlor grate, his gray hair untidy as though he had been sweeping his hands through it. "How is my sister-in-law?"

"Moll Bacon is nursing her now, sir. I'm to make a medicinal tea from this." I held up the little cloth bag.

"Don't show it to me! Be about it, then."

I bowed my head, grinding my teeth at his snappish tone. "Yes, sir."

The kitchen stove was dark and cold, of course. I was used to attending to it, though, because Mrs. Worth was so near with a shilling that she refused to hire anyone to help me around the house—though I had heard gossips in the street say that her husband had left her very well set, with not only the house and land but a steady income from his investments in ships and trade. As quickly as I could, I raked out the white and gray ashes from the wood-box into the ash scuttle, then piled in some brown and sharp-scented pine shavings as tinder. Atop that I built a small pyramid of kindling—splints of more pine, which would catch easy and burn fast—and then, to weigh that down, a few hickory logs. I got the tinderbox and struck fire with it, then set a splinter alight and touched it to the wood shavings until they were burning. The kindling began to crackle, and the fragrant pine sap started to ooze and flow. I put in two more lengths of hickory and closed the wood-box door. The stove top would be hot in a matter of minutes.

While it heated, I went out to the well and drew a pail of fresh water. The hens came clustering around me, wanting to be fed, and the rooster perched on top of the coop, flapped his wings, and crowed piercingly, and I imagined him proclaiming, *Day, it's day, it's day, it's da-a-a-y!* Filled, the water pail was heavy, and I had to use two hands to carry it back to the kitchen, taking care not to splash it out as I waded through the impatient chickens. I used the late Mr. Worth's pint beer mug to measure the water into the cast-iron teapot and then put the pot on to boil. Mr. Richard had come to the doorway. "Child, don't be idle! Make me a bit of breakfast while I wait."

"Yes, sir."

I scrambled two eggs in butter and fried a nice slice of bread. By then the teapot was bubbling, so I dropped in the little cloth bag. Mr. Richard sat at the table and ate the bread and eggs, drinking only water that he dipped from the pail. His brother, Mrs. Worth's husband, had been a sailor and a sea captain, used to drinking pale ale with breakfast and a glass of rum mixed with water with dinner, but Mr. Richard abstained from all alcohol except a little glass of wine now and then. He served as a deacon in the Congregational Church, and I knew full well that he had never approved of his older brother's ways or habits. I stood by the stove with my chin down, murmuring under my breath.

"What are you doing?" he growled at me. "Praying?"

"Counting," I said, skipping from fifty to fifty-two because I had paused to speak.

"Better for you to pray," he muttered. "Where is that son of mine?"

He did not expect me to answer, and so I didn't, simply going on in my count until I whispered "one hundred" to myself and took the kettle off the stove. I went to the parlor to look at the clock. The minute hand stood at six minutes before the hour.

I had time to eat. Back in the kitchen I fried a little piece of bread for myself and cut a small wedge of cheese from the hoop in the pantry. Mr. Richard pushed away from the table and left me alone as he returned restlessly to the parlor. I finished the bread and cheese, then put our dishes and the frying pan into the wash basin.

In the front parlor, where Mr. Richard stood moodily in front of the fire he had built, staring down into it with his hands clasped behind him, I checked the clock again. The minute hand now touched eight minutes after the hour. I waited until it nicked off another minute, and then I went back to the kitchen. As Moll had directed, I poured the tea into the mug—it was a dark greenish-brown liquid, smelling faintly of licorice—and threw the sodden bag of herbs into the slop pail.

Mrs. Worth looked a little calmer when I brought the tea into the bedroom. "Here we are," said Moll. "Drink this down. It will do you good."

"Where is Richard?" asked Mrs. Worth querulously as she struggled to sit up in bed, propped against both of her pillows.

"He is down in the parlor," I told her. "I made breakfast for him."

"You gave him my food?" she demanded with a cross glance. "What did he eat, and how much?"

"Just two eggs and a slice of bread."

"Remember that," she said, shaking a bony finger at me. "He will have to repay me!" She took a little, cautious sip of the tea and made a sour face at the taste of it.

"I should attend to my chores," I said to Moll, in a small voice.

Mrs. Worth drank the rest of the liquid from the mug, making "Gahh!" sounds after each noisy swallow. "Go," Moll said to me. "I don't need you here right now. But boil more water."

I put more water on the stove, went out and fed the chickens, and then came back inside. With part of the heated water I washed and rinsed the dishes. Then I dried and put them away and threw the dishpan of still-steaming water out into the side yard. The sun was well up now, the day breezy, with scudding raggedy gray and white clouds now and then dimming the light. I went on to my other daily chores, dusting and sweeping, scouring the front steps, and so on. Just before noon Mr. Richard told me to go next door to see if his son, David, was home and to tell him to come over if he was.

"Next door," he said, but it was a little walk away, for here the houses were not close-packed, as they were in the heart of town. I tapped on the back door of Mr. Richard's two-story home—a small house only when compared to his brother's three-story one; Mr. Richard said that an earthly mansion was nothing but a sinful vanity that the Lord would punish in due time—and Mr. David answered on my second knock.

He was twenty-two years old, not very tall but thin, like his father, with a head of thick, curly, auburn-brown hair and quick, darting brown eyes. "Patience," he said. "How is my aunt?"

"Sick and in bed, sir," I replied. "Your father asks that you come over."

★"True to the young teen's viewpoint, this taut, eloquent first novel will make readers feel . . . the seething fury and desperation over the daily discrimination that drove the oppressed to fight back."

—*BOOKLIST*, STARRED REVIEW

THE ROCK AND THE RIVER

Will Sam choose to be the Rock or the River?

FROM

ALADDIN

PUBLISHED BY SIMON & SCHUSTER

CURL UP WITH A GOOD MYSTERY!

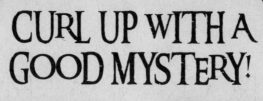

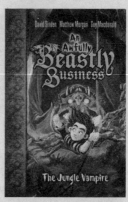

From Aladdin

Published by Simon & Schuster